Secret Lives

Secret Lives

Caroline Macdonald

SIMON & SCHUSTER

BOOKS FOR

YOUNG READERS

SIMON & SCHUSTER BOOKS FOR YOUNG READERS
An imprint of Simon & Schuster Children's Publishing Division
1230 Avenue of the Americas, New York, New York 10020
Copyright © 1993 by Caroline Macdonald
All rights reserved including the right of reproduction
in whole or in part in any form. Originally published in Australia by
Omnibus Books, a division of the ASHTON SCHOLASTIC GROUP.
First American Edition, 1995.
SIMON & SCHUSTER BOOKS FOR YOUNG READERS
is a trademark of Simon & Schuster.

The text for this book is set in 11-point Galliard.
Manufactured in the United States of America

10 9 8 7 6 5 4 3 2 1

Library of Congress Cataloging-in-Publication Data
Macdonald, Caroline.
      Secret lives / Caroline Macdonald.
            p. cm.
      Summary: A fifteen-year-old Australian boy creates a character for a
school writing project, and when the character comes to life he discovers that
he must confront his past before he can lay the character to rest.
      ISBN 0-671-51081-9
      [1. Authorship—Fiction. 2. Grandparents—Fiction.] I. Title.
PZ7.M14644Se   1995   [Fic]—dc20   94-24507

For Erica, as always

You are my creator,
but I am your master; obey!
—Mary Shelley, *Frankenstein*

Part One

Gideon

The spectral Gideon came into my life on the first Monday of the holidays. I was hooked, right from the beginning.

I'm not sure why he appeared so soon. Perhaps it was because my two closest friends had gone skiing in Victoria with their parents, and I had nothing planned for the two-week break. The days hadn't started their sudden slither toward the new term, so that before you know it you're back to school tomorrow, holiday projects still not started.

His name, Gideon, came first. At that stage he was still an indistinct presence, no more than a group of impressions. The strongest impression was his difference in appearance from me. Total opposite, really.

I was then three months shy of fifteen years old, an Australian male descended from Scots/Irish people who'd migrated to the southern hemisphere in the last century, lured by the goldfields. I was sandy-haired—flyaway hair, quite long—with pale skin that reddened both from the sun in the summertime and the winter cold. Tall for my age, thin, with large feet and hands; I was also a limper. My left knee had been smashed in a car accident that should be ancient and forgotten history, except that the knee joint had never been reconstructed properly. Successive operations hadn't fixed it.

I could do most things. I was good at swimming and I belonged to a rowing club. But fast team sports were out, and also things like skateboarding where your legs do a twisting movement, and probably skiing, although I'd never tried it—I simply fell over, which hurt, in all sorts of ways. Sometimes, on bad days, I had to use a walking stick. Jaz said the walking stick gave me an interesting style. It was kind of her to say that, but it definitely wasn't the image I wanted.

Gideon was older than me, maybe seventeen. He had dark glossy hair and fine-textured olive skin, strong-looking black straight eyebrows, a thin face. I didn't think he was black, really; if so I wasn't sure yet what race. He hadn't spoken so far. I didn't know what his voice would be like. I realized suddenly the importance of people's voices and how much we learn from the words they choose.

He was wearing dark jeans, a soft leather bomber jacket over a plain white silky shirt buttoned to the neck. Plain leather shoes, not Reeboks or anything else with words on them. I guessed that he would never wear clothes with writing.

That day I was wearing the same as usual. Checked shirt hanging out over a T-shirt over blue jeans washed till they were soft and pale. My T-shirt would have had some jokey slogan like MY SON SENT ME THIS FROM FLORIDA or SOUTH AUSTRALIAN ROWING CLUB OLD-AGE PENSIONERS' DIVISION. And, of course, I wore sneakers that advertised themselves.

Gideon walked in silently. He slouched, hands hooked on his jeans pockets. He didn't look at me at first but perched on the arm of the easy chair by the window and contemplated my room. I didn't mind. The Christmas holidays before, I'd given my room a lot of thought and action. I was proud of it. It was all done with paint.

The floor and the bottom part of the walls were navy blue, a color so dark it was nearly black. Then the walls were shaded through dark blue to light blue to just below the ceiling, where they became pure white, as was the ceiling itself.

I painted the furniture the same way—the desk, the chair, the window blind, cupboards, wardrobe, bedframe, each shaded to match the floor and the wall it stood against. One problem was the word processor, a gray blot against the midnight blue; the paint wouldn't stick to the plastic and I was afraid that the globs that formed would glue up the keyboard. I found a blue cloth to cover both the VDU and the printer.

I was trying to get the effect of open space above my head, maybe a kind of infinity: space to think, not a restricting enclosure. It sort of worked, particularly if I half closed my eyes so that the paintwork was blurred. I knew it wasn't a very professional job. There were roller marks and patchy areas where the color hadn't shaded smoothly.

Lil gave me the dark blue easy chair, and we dyed sheets and a couple of duvet covers so my bed blended into the wall. She lost points, however, when she suggested I paint a cloud on one of the walls. I had trouble explaining it wasn't meant to represent something real like sky; it was symbolic, somehow. Symbolic headspace.

And now Gideon was in here. His presence was so strong by now that the air shook.

He unhooked his right hand and touched his chin lightly. He had long thin hands. The skin at his knuckles was darker than the rest. I noticed that the knuckle at the base of his little finger was grazed.

"Not bad," he said.

Not. Bad. Too few words to establish much about him. The first word was clipped, the "t" hardly sounded; the second drawled so it verged on two syllables.

"Not a bad room." (I was right. He had a drawly voice.) "I can see it as a scene for a murder."

A murder? Whose? I'd thought about many things in this room, but never a murder.

"A splatter murder. Lots of blood."

What was he—some kind of movie director? But I could almost see the effect: the splashes of blood becoming brighter red as the blue faded.

He stood up and for a moment he was a silhouette against the strong light from the window.

"Whose murder? Yours, perhaps." I was sure he was smiling. "Frightened?"

Of course I wasn't frightened. Why should I have been?

Lil

I lived with Lil in a crumbling brick and stone house in Adelaide. The garden at the back was ancient and overgrown and spider-ridden. "There's no point in hacking and taming the garden," Lil said, "because the spiders will shift into the house." There was a clear area paved with greening bricks where we had a wooden table and some old kitchen chairs. Lil liked to sit there on sunny afternoons, dreaming up ideas for TV soap operas.

My room was at the back of the house, the northwest corner, and its window looked out on this garden. Lil's room was at the front, the southwest corner. Between our rooms were the bathroom and the small room that was mine when I was little, before my parents died. Now it was a storeroom for things like suitcases and spare duvets.

The rest of the house, the east side, was simple: one long living room running from front to back, with a grand old fireplace near one end and sofas and a big dining table, and a gas heater on the wall near the kitchen area at the back.

Lil was my grandmother, my father's mother. Often things about her reminded me of my father. Physically she was tall and thin, as he was and I would be, too. She had his same recklessness about being proper. I remembered my mother using stronger, harsher words than "recklessness." Lil had passed on to my father her Irish-dark hair and eyes while I had inherited my mother's lighter coloring, along with, I'd always feared, her greater suspicion and caution about the world.

Lil kept her hair cut short, and the silver wings at each side didn't make her look old, just dramatic. People who didn't know about my parents assumed she was my mother.

Her name was Lilian Ganty, and I'd always called her Lil. She required it. Titles, she said, like "Granny" or "Mom," pushed people into roles and made other people expect certain things of them. Probably it was significant that I used to call my father Pat but my mother was always Mom, never Elaine.

Lil wasn't actually old, thirty-four years older than me, not even fifty then. The result of very young pregnancies, she told me. "Watch out, Ian, they run in the family." She was sixteen and single when she gave birth to my father, Pat. She'd been sent off to a convent to keep her secret, but not her baby, who was adopted into a childless Catholic family.

Lil told me she'd managed to cope with this separation from her baby because while she'd been hidden in the convent during her pregnancy, she'd become close friends with one of the young nuns, Sister Mary Menchua. They kept on writing to each other, and Sister Mary Menchua sent Lil small pieces of news about her lost boy.

By the time Pat was thirteen, the news reports changed.

His adoptive family was having problems with him. Pat had been quite good at schoolwork, but now he was getting bad grades because he hardly ever turned up for classes. His parents gave him everything he wanted but he shoplifted. He was "running with wild boys."

Lil quoted this phrase with a cynical twist to her mouth. They, she said, meaning the adoptive parents, would call a boy wild if he farted before breakfast. They reacted by sending Pat to a strict and expensive boarding school.

Lil went to Italy and London for a year, studying to upgrade her teaching qualifications. When she got back to Adelaide, she decided to find Pat, who was by then seventeen years old.

She knew which school he went to. He was nearing the end of his final year. She found him on the point of being expelled, charged with a number of wild-boy acts. But the crime that enraged the authorities most, the act that meant that Lil, at the age of thirty-three, was about to be a grandmother, was that Elaine Duncan, the twenty-four-year-old tutor in math to nonachieving middle-school boys, was five months pregnant with Pat's child. Me.

It wasn't only the school authorities who were enraged. Elaine's parents were speechless with horror. "They," Pat's adoptive parents, were heartbroken and defeated. Lil took center stage.

All this was fascinating to me. I wanted moment-to-moment dialogue, the unfolding of events.

"When I first saw him," Lil said, "I was unhinged. It was like finding a piece of myself, but so separate, so precious, that I didn't deserve it. If I made one false move I'd lose it. I was terrified that I'd say something wrong. Or somehow be wrong." Apparently she didn't make the mistakes she feared. Pat allied himself with her very quickly. She met Elaine, who wanted both Pat and the baby. Lil rented this house, and they moved in. So I was born here.

Well, at the hospital, but this is where I first lived and grew up.

So, that was Lil. Fragments of her, anyway. Ours was an unusual household; I knew that even when I was little. Then suddenly Pat and Elaine were gone, and there was just Lil and me. And ST, our wandering terrier.

And now there was Gideon, too.

He was starting to take control from that first Monday.

• • •

Lil was going to Victor Harbor for a few days to attend a teachers' conference. I was supposed to stay with Zelda, a cousin of Lil's who lived a couple of blocks away.

I didn't want to go to Zelda's. I wanted to stay here.

"Well, don't go," said Gideon.

It was Monday, late afternoon. Lil and I were folding the laundry still warm from the dryer. I knew she was ready to leave. If I was going to argue the case for staying here, I'd have to start now.

"Don't say anything to her," said Gideon. "Just do it."

In a few moments Lil was jingling the car keys and hitching on her shoulder bag. She was wearing faded black jeans and her favorite long sweater. It was inside out for some reason and the label at the back of her neck showed. I was wondering if I should get the scissors and offer to clip it off but it was too late—she was saying good-bye, a quick kiss on my forehead and out the door.

Zelda would be expecting me. I whistled for ST, locked the front door and walked the short distance to her house.

Jaz answered the door. Jaz was Zelda's daughter, and I'd known her all my life. She was the one who said comforting things about my walking stick. She was about two years older than me, and she was very serious. She didn't smile or laugh very much, and she stared steadily at you when you spoke. She always blinked very slowly.

"I'm glad it's only you," she said. She was wearing her

reading glasses and held a pencil. Her words meant she was busy doing something and didn't want to talk. "Come in. You know where your room is."

"Jaz, hang on. I'm not coming to stay. I'm just stopping by to say I'll be at home, with ST, because . . ."

She knew—I could tell by her almost-smile—that for reasons of my own I didn't want to be sent off to baby-sitters. "When's she back?" she asked.

"Thursday morning."

"I'll bring over some takeout on Wednesday night," she said. "Date?"

"Okay."

ST led the way home. She was called Social Terrier because whenever there was a party within a four block radius, or even people having a couple of friends over for lunch, ST turned up and pretended to be the family dog. If we lost her for more than a few hours we looked around for a house that had more cars parked outside than usual.

It was dark and I was hungry. I looked in the fridge. There was part of a cooked chicken but it looked pale and chilly so I gave some to ST who didn't want it either. I phoned for a Hawaiian pizza and turned on the TV.

Gideon's Car

"Television," Gideon said. He said it mockingly. He despised ordinary things, simple pleasures like relaxing on the sofa, stomach full of pizza, watching an early evening soap opera with a book to read during the commercials.

He sprawled on an armchair and watched for a few minutes. "Predictable stuff, isn't it," he said. "I bet she sees him with that other girl and gets the wrong idea. But she won't say anything. She'll just give him the cold treatment."

He was right, of course. It was like watching TV with Lil.

"You've got all this freedom, accountable to no one, and you're blobbed out in front of the TV."

What did he expect me to be doing on a cold Monday night? If Jake and Lin weren't away skiing, the three of us would probably be doing just this, lazing around, talking, TV on.

"Let's go out. Somewhere. Doesn't matter. Not the movies. Just out."

His voice wasn't drawly now. It was in short hurried sentences. He was by the door, then out on the veranda.

I grabbed my wallet and the house keys, and locked the door behind me. We walked for a block along the narrow sidewalk, he a few paces ahead of me, ducking the overhanging branches of the gums and silver birches planted along the curb. We rounded a corner. The air was freezing.

"Doesn't matter about the cold," he said. "I've got a car."

A car? I hadn't known that detail.

"That one." It was a Holden automatic, a bit like Lil's but about ten generations newer. Gideon had left the keys in the ignition. The car smelled new and clean, almost perfumed. Just before I got my door closed, there was a blur of movement and ST was on my knee. Yes. Dog—that was the smell I was used to in Lil's car.

"Don't you ever wash your dog?" Gideon was driving slowly, easing the car around the next corner. ST didn't like water so we always put off washing her for as long as possible.

Gideon switched on the headlights. We were heading for the traffic lights at the intersection. Another set of lights and we were on Greenhill Road. Swerving among the traffic to get into a right-hand lane. Cars tooting because Gideon didn't bother to use the signals. "Stuff them," he said.

We shot along King William Street, near the city center now, still swinging from lane to lane. Left into Hindley Street. Gideon slowed, looking at the people drifting along the sidewalks. "Dead," he said. "Let's go to the Port."

He made a horrendous right turn in the face of oncoming traffic. Again there was a chorus of outraged car horns. I wondered if he was used to driving in the city. He seemed to be surviving on sheer nerve.

Finally we were on Port Road, where Gideon had three lanes to dodge in. Where did he learn to drive—in a circus? Lil had given me some lessons on deserted back roads in the country near Murray Bridge last Christmas. Who had taught him to drive? Did he have a family, brothers, sisters? Who were his friends? Where did he live? There was a lot I still had to work out.

I think we both heard it at the same time, the wailing siren, and in the side mirror I saw the blue flash of a police car. Gideon hit the accelerator. The traffic lights ahead were green, yellow. We shot through the intersection as the red appeared. The police car behind us had to hesitate for ages while the cross-traffic dithered about giving it the right of way. Then the cops were through.

We were going faster, weaving right and left through gaps in the traffic. Sixty miles an hour, seventy, more. I breathed deeply to control my waves of panic and excitement. We were flying, and it was great. The blue flash was flying, too, maybe even faster.

Gideon swung sharply into a side street. "I think it's time to abandon ship, wouldn't you agree?"

Did he really say that? It sounded like a line from a World War II movie. I didn't have time to think about it. I had the door open and was out before the car stopped. I rolled over a couple of times and stood up, hearing a scrape of metal as the car slid into a concrete power pole several houses away. Gideon had disappeared, dropped into hiding, become a shadow, and that was what I had to do, too. I tried to run, screaming inside as my knee slid out of joint, and fell among some industrial bins and ugly shrubs.

All this took maybe two seconds or three. I felt ST's

tongue on my chin at the same time as the police car shot around the corner.

Because the police waited to check that no one was injured inside the car, I had time to disappear. I managed to limp through a labyrinth of shop-back areas to the side entrance of a late-night deli. ST led the way, lured by the sound of voices. By the time I caught up, she was leaping among four people waiting for cigarettes and newspapers. "Get that dog outta my shop!" the florid man behind the counter was shouting.

I did. The deli was on Port Road. I tucked my head down and limped fast in the direction of the city. I was a long way from home. My knee hurt. The good thing was that my wallet and house keys were still in my pocket. Inside my wallet was a five-dollar bill, and a two-dollar coin, and a bit of other change. It was what was left from the pizza, paid for with my last twenty dollars.

The first taxi driver I flagged down didn't mind about taking ST in his car, as long as I held her on my knees. He took me the whole way home for only nine dollars. Maybe he felt sorry for me.

Pat

I felt sorry for myself, anyway. When I woke up the next morning I ached. My palms were grazed from hitting the sidewalk and my knee felt worse than it had all year. Without these signs, the ride in Gideon's car would have been hard to believe.

I went back to bed, lay on my back, and waited for the room's shading to have its effect, to lift my brain up and away from the aches and pains of my body. I was impatient to know more about Gideon. His background. What he was doing now.

He was in Rundle Mall, turning over a couple of coins in his fingers. He went into a phone booth. I heard the phone ring—it was the real phone in the living room. Unwillingly I got up and answered it.

"Ian? Hi." It was Jaz. "Um . . . just letting you know ST's over here."

"Yeah?" So what? ST visited Jaz and Zelda nearly every morning.

"Um . . ." Jaz sounded hesitant. "Everything okay?"

"Yeah, why not?"

"It's just that . . ." Jaz was hesitating again. I knew there was something she had to say. She wouldn't have phoned just about ST. "Well, last night there were all these cop cars zooming around so I phoned to see if you were okay. Um . . . sorry . . . I know it sounds really intrusive. . . ." I didn't reply when she paused. "Well, you weren't there. Then Zelda found out the only reason the cops were around was because of some stolen car. Nothing, really."

"Yeah? I missed all that."

She paused again. Was she going to ask straight out where I'd been? No, of course she wouldn't. Not Jaz's style.

"So I thought maybe Lil told you not to answer the phone if you were there on your own at night."

"Of course she didn't!" Lil didn't issue orders like that. "I just went out for a while. I took ST for a long walk."

"Really? In the freezing cold dark?"

"I just felt like it." Why was I explaining myself so much? "You know, into town."

"I see," she said slowly. Again a silence. "Well, watch out for bogeymen, Ian," she went on. "ST's not much of a bodyguard."

"Yeah." After I'd hung up I stared at the phone for a few minutes. The handpiece was beaded with moisture where I'd been gripping it. I felt reprimanded, ticked off. Humiliated. Then I was angry. Jaz wasn't even seventeen yet. I really used to admire her. I thought we were friends. It was no part of our friendship that she told me off.

Gideon understood. "Who does she think she is—your mother or something?" He grinned. "If she only knew . . ."

That spun me backward through time. "If she only knew" were Pat's words; "she" was Elaine, my mother.

In the dresser where the phone stood there was a deep drawer filled with photographs. They were all taken in those years from when I appeared only as a growing bulge inside my mother's oversized shirts through to when I was twelve, when Pat and Elaine weren't around anymore. It was as if Lil thought that seventeen years of missed photo-taking had to be packed into those first years.

The early photos were carefully tucked in date order between clear plastic in large photo albums, some with dates and descriptions in my mother's handwriting. It seemed she lost the inspiration after a while—maybe when she started to realize that marriage to Pat was hard work. Anyway, the photos from the time I was four or five were left in their original envelopes.

It was the photos of Pat I wanted to see again, particularly the early ones. I'd known, but wanted to check, that he looked nothing like Gideon. Pat had a long face and neck, a wide mouth that was usually partway open with laughter in these photos. His hair was dark like Gideon's but different: wavy, swept back from a high forehead. In the early photos, the ones where I was a bulge, his hair was still boarding-school neat and short, but it was longer in every photo since then. Pat looked thin and loose-limbed, almost gawky in comparison with the compact shape of Gideon.

I was relieved. I didn't want there to be similarities between my father and Gideon. I didn't want to be drawing comparisons, making interpretations of Gideon based on my memories of Pat.

It was just that Gideon had used those words of Pat's from years ago, *if she only knew*. I had just turned seven years old. Pat and I were going into town. I was excited. I adored going out with Pat. There was always some sort of adventure before we got home.

Elaine had given Pat fifty-six dollars in an envelope to pick up two textbooks she'd ordered, plus a few extra dollars for us to have a snack at the café across the road from the book-shop. This didn't seem strange to me, this way she treated

Pat and me equally as two little kids to be sent on errands with instructions and counted-out money in an envelope.

Pat found a spot for Lil's old VW right outside the café so we went there first. We sat at one of the tables outside. My passion then was for chocolate gelati with whipped cream. I loved the way the cream was hardened by the coldness of the ice cream. One cone never seemed to be enough. Pat's eyes gleamed with the challenge. He went inside and got me another. Then another.

Halfway through the third one I stopped. I didn't know what was happening to me, only that in a split second I was going to explode. I swung to the side and then projectile vomited over the woman at the next table. I still remember how it sprang out of me with the force of water from a fire-fighter's hose.

"Oh lord," said Pat. Half laughing, he grabbed my arm and pushed me, still green and trembling and heaving, into the car. He fell into the driver's seat as the woman, gasping, brushed her dripping jacket and skirt with her fingers. In his haste Pat, never a good driver, backed into the car behind. The car's owner was at another outside table. Both he and the woman approached us and we were trapped.

You couldn't even see the dent on the old VW but the other car had a smashed and crumpled headlight. Pat had to give the car owner Lil's name and address. Then the woman made us drive her to an expensive hotel on North Terrace where she was staying, and where there was a one-hour dry cleaner. "You were being irresponsible," she kept saying to Pat. "I saw you stuffing that child with ice cream."

Pat had to pay for the dry cleaning. It was a silk suit, needing special care, and there was a shirt as well. Forty-nine dollars. Pat handed over the textbook money. I was still feeling sick. "You need some fresh air and so does the car," said Pat. He drove around the corner, parked illegally near the park. We opened all the car windows and then went for a walk beside the river.

I felt better immediately. I raced along the bank of the Torrens, scattering ducks and plovers. When we got back to the car, there was a parking ticket under the windshield wiper. Pat crumpled it and threw it in the gutter.

"Your books haven't arrived," Pat told Elaine when we got home. She frowned and then caught sight of my shoes, my brand new blue-and-white seventh-birthday first-ever pair of Reeboks. They were brown and green now, crusted with river mud and duck poo.

"Why do you have to bring him back in such a mess?" she demanded. "You're only out for an hour and a half and look at his shoes. They're ruined."

"They'll clean up okay," Pat said, a question in his voice. I hoped they would. We didn't have much money. Pat was unemployed, and Elaine was studying full-time for a master's degree. I didn't have any idea what that was then, except that it meant we had to keep the house quiet. We lived on Lil's part-time teaching salary. Buying the Reeboks had been an effort, Elaine had told me. I felt chastened about the shoes, guilty I hadn't looked after them better.

Elaine held out her hand while I took my shoes off, and then she disappeared into the laundry with them. It was then that Pat whispered to me, with a grin, "If she only knew . . ."

Of course she found out. There was the missing book money, then the summons for the parking offense and the bill for three hundred dollars from the other driver's insurance company.

I heard Pat telling Lil about it shortly after Elaine had cleaned my shoes and gone back into her room, door closed, to work. Lil was snorting with laughter before he was halfway through. She said the laugh was worth the expense. Elaine didn't see it that way, and there was a big row.

That was the pattern I remember—Lil and Pat always seeing eye to eye, Elaine growing farther apart from them, me bobbing in the gulf between.

Well, it was all resolved by the accident in the air over the Pacific Ocean. Elaine and Pat and many other passengers were never seen again.

Encounter

I was stuffing the photos back into the drawer when the phone rang again. It was Grandmother Duncan, Elaine's mother. Instantly I was on guard.

"Ian, darling," she said. She called everyone "darling," except Grandfather Duncan. "How are things going? Are you having a marvelous school break?"

"It's okay," I said.

"Well, your grandfather and I have spent the morning in the garden, and just finished lunch, and we thought we'd pop over and see you and Lilian."

Lunch? I looked at my watch, astonished. I'd spent hours over the photos. Grandmother Duncan was going on about cuttings from the garden Lilian might like to plant.

"Lil's away."

"Away? Ian, darling, she hasn't left you on your own?"

"Er . . . no." I was thinking fast. Already I could see her kick-starting Grandfather Duncan into action to race around here and carry me off to safety, as she'd see it. "I'm staying around the corner. I'm just here to pick up some gear for rowing practice."

"Oh," she said, "I see. Oh well. I'll pop the cuttings in water and hope they'll survive. When does Lilian get back, darling?"

"Thursday, I think. I'll get her to call you."

"If you would. Now, you're sure you're all right?"

"Yeah. Sure. Bye."

There had been bitter words between Lil and the Grandparents Duncan over my upbringing after the first shock of my parents' death. For me it was like another nightmare unfolding, the threat of having to leave Lil and go to live with the Duncans. They attempted to adopt me legally, saying things like they could provide a more secure environment for me in these uncertain economic times, and that they were a married couple in an established *home*—in other words, criticizing Lil.

Lil was determined to keep me and didn't care how dirty she played. She reminded them how they'd urged Elaine to have a swift abortion when they discovered she was pregnant from a schoolboy. If they'd had their way, I wouldn't even exist. Grandmother Duncan didn't know that I knew that.

"I had a grandmother like that, once," Gideon said. "I disconnected her brake cable and she drove over a cliff."

I wasn't sure whether to believe this. But I was getting more background information about Gideon. There was family trouble and it had something to do with why Gideon left school at fifteen, but what that reason was I didn't know yet. As for friends: he liked girls, and they found him attractive. They said he was exotic, different in the way he dressed and spoke. He didn't run with a pack. Tough but not a hoodlum. Yet he'd never had any relationships that continued beyond one date.

Male friends: he had a few, but he'd lost common interest with most school friends once he left. Workmates? What was his job? How did he earn money, buy clothes?

"Job?" he said. "You must be joking. What jobs?"

Yes. What jobs. There weren't that many around even for people who finished school.

"That is," he went on, "if you mean nine-to-five paycheck tax-taken-out kind of jobs."

I knew he wasn't referring to an alternative of, say, volunteer work at the local child care center. This was leading to Gideon-as-outlaw.

I decided to leave these questions for a while, even though the Gideon investigation was gathering a kind of compulsive momentum for me.

I looked past my word processor to the window beyond. The day was nearly over and I had rowing practice. That hadn't been a lie to Grandmother Duncan; I'd just altered the time by a few hours. It wasn't really rowing practice, on the water that is, because half the club was away for the holidays. But our club had a group booking at a gymnasium on Tuesday nights from six o'clock for fitness training. I liked the workouts. Sam, one of the trainers there, kept a watch on my knee and gave me a schedule for it. The way it felt today, it needed some special care.

I checked that I had enough coins for the bus trip to North Terrace and back. Just. Then that was all my money gone till Lil came back.

"Like a lift in my car?" Gideon murmured as I collected my gym gear.

"No," I said loudly. I didn't even want to think about Gideon's car. "No," I said to ST, "you're definitely not coming," and I shut her in the house, securing the cat-flap so she couldn't follow me, and walked to the bus stop.

By the time I got off the bus near the railway station it was dusk. I was running late, but all the same I lingered, smelling the pie cart, remembering I hadn't eaten all day. I stood on the corner, balancing my hunger against the need to keep enough money for the bus home. A pie after the gym, I decided. Sam would lend me enough for a pie. Then I saw Lil. I couldn't believe it was her at first. She was half a block away, outside the casino entrance, and she was walking toward the corner. I stepped back, instinctively knowing she wouldn't want to see me right now. I couldn't believe it was her because of the way she looked.

She was like a model in a magazine. That was the impression I got in that instant before I backed out of sight. She wore a black tight-fitting dress and a long silvery floaty something over it. Her eyes—loaded with makeup—looked huge. She was with a man.

I must have been mistaken. It *had* to be someone who just looked like her. I peered around the corner again. She stood with her back to me, near the sleek cars on the casino parking area. The man was a dark-suit type, leaning attentively toward her as she spoke. I drew back as they got into a white car.

A few seconds later the car drove out of the intersection and eased into the traffic on North Terrace. "Follow her," Gideon said.

How could I? No money for a cab, no car—

The rush hour traffic was thick. The car carrying Lil waited at the traffic light. A bus was edging away from the curb, its passenger door still open. I hitched my gym bag over my shoulder and made a leap for it.

"You can't get on. I've left the stop," shouted the driver. I exaggerated my limp, dragging myself up the steps, and he said no more, shifting his concentration to forcing the bus into the slow-moving traffic.

The bus was full. From where I stood at the front I could watch Lil's car. The heavy traffic was keeping everyone crawling.

The woman in the seat nearest to where I stood nudged my arm and I noticed that my gym bag was almost in her ear. I apologized and dumped it on the floor. "I'm not sure if I'm on the right bus. Where are we going?"

"It's the Magill Road express."

"That's a relief," I said. Was it? Who knew where Lil was going in that car? I was sure that Gideon's "follow her" hadn't meant by bus. It seemed an insane idea now, and he wasn't here to help me.

The Trip

On Magill Road the traffic thinned, and when the bus made its first stop to release passengers, the white car kept moving. In a moment its taillights were indistinguishable from others.

A few stops later the bus was half empty. I slumped down in the seat behind the driver and looked at the reflection of my face in the window beside me. "Hello, stupid," I said.

"What's that?" said the driver.

Sharp ears. "Talking to myself," I said. "I'm on the wrong bus. Do you go back to the city?"

"There's a few minutes' wait at the top of the road. Then I go back to the city. It's a roundabout route, though."

"Will I have to pay again?"

"Probably," he said. "But . . . maybe not if you stay on board."

Eventually the bus turned off the road and on to a tree-lined area. The driver switched the engine off and stood up. His back was to me. He was short and heavily built, bulging above his trouser belt. He stretched with his elbows struck out at shoulder level, head back, yawning.

"Don't move. There's a gun pointed at the arse end of your spine." It was a voice from the back of the bus, a cold and flat voice that wasn't joking. The driver froze, his elbows in the air.

I was frightened. I stayed unmoving, slumped in the seat, hoping I'd get away with being invisible until all this was over.

"I want the money. Don't do anything stupid. Move very slowly and open up the money box."

The driver breathed out heavily, making a small sound with it, a slight groan that said *oh no, not again*. His elbows dropped.

"There isn't any money. Just a bit of change. People use cards these days and prepaid tickets . . ."

The driver was still facing forward, speaking to the reflection of the gunman in the rearview mirror. I realized the driver would be able to see me, too. I cringed lower in the seat. Surely he wouldn't want me to do something heroic?

"Don't shit me. Get moving." Why didn't someone see what was going on? There were cars passing, and surely people in the houses across the road. But maybe it wouldn't look suspicious: the driver stretching, talking to a passenger in the back.

"Open the money box. Give the cash to that kid in the front. Shovel it into the bag he's carrying." He'd known I was there all the time.

I saw the driver shift his stare to me in the reflection. Then he shrugged. "Open up the bag," he said.

My hands were shaking. I fumbled at the zipper of my bag then held it open. A faint scent of the gym floated out and I wished I'd gone there. Or stayed home.

The driver tossed in a couple of handfuls of silver, a few dollar and two-dollar coins. He lifted the change compartment and added two five-dollar bills. "That's it," he said.

"And your wallet."

"Come on! I don't carry cash on me. Do you think I'm crazy?"

"Sure you do. I can see that fat old wallet bulging from here. Reach into the man's jacket, kid."

I was standing up now, my eyes level with the driver's. His mouth was tight with fury. His strong arms hung loose, huge meaty hands with curled fingers. I thought he'd throttle me. I decided I wasn't going to touch his jacket.

"Give him the wallet."

The driver slowly, slowly lifted his right hand, reached into his inside pocket, brought out a brown plastic wallet. His eyes did not leave mine. "You little bastard," he said as I took it from him. It was stuffed with a fold of bills. I saw the blue-gray of hundred-dollar bills.

"Into the bag. Good lad. Now bring it here."

I turned and saw the gunman for the first time. He wore a black knitted thing over his head, making his face into a frightening mask with two small glittering holes to see through and a wider space for his mouth. He stood by the center door, a big man in a black coat.

My legs wouldn't work.

"Move it!"

All I could see during that endless walk toward the dark figure was the shiny circular end of the gun barrel. Every time I lurched sideways as my knee gave out, the gun followed, stayed aimed at my face. I had no thoughts of doing anything heroic. I was terrified.

Then, suddenly, the gunman's left hand shot forward

and grabbed the bag before I was ready. He was out the door and running. The momentum of his grab dragged me after him and I tripped. For the second time in twenty-four hours, I hit the gravel.

I must have passed out. When I opened my eyes, I was in darkness, and the bus had gone.

• • •

It was the absence of the bus that confused me. I sat on the gravel for several minutes trying to piece together what had happened. My head throbbed, and when I touched my face, I found stickiness on my fingers.

There'd been a hold-up on the bus, right, and the gunman had escaped. The driver must have gone off to get help without seeing me there. God. He might have driven over me.

I stood up creakily and found I could walk fairly well. The second fall must have pushed my knee back in joint, which was good, because I had a long way to go.

Of course I should find the nearest police station and report as a witness. And I'd been robbed as well—gym bag, track pants and top, towel, the paperback I'd been reading.

I walked along Magill Road toward the city. I'd never been inside a police station in my life, never had anything to do with the police. But I'd seen "Hill Street Blues" and "The Bill," and I knew enough.

There'd be a dozy desk-person who wouldn't believe me and who'd try to get rid of me. Then a higher ranking officer would overhear my story.

This is a top priority investigation and you're our number one witness, he/she would say.

I'd be taken to a warm little room and given a cup of tea. They'd record my account of events and my descriptions. Take my address and phone number, so I could be a witness at the trial, or even identify the criminal in a line-up. Line-ups are always tense and exciting moments in police dramas. And also so they could phone my parents to come and pick me up.

I live with my grandmother.

Your granny. Can she drive?

Of course she can drive! (Lil was right about titles.) She's not home right now.

When will she be home?

About Thursday.

She's left you on your own?!

Just lend me ten dollars for a taxi.

Hang on a minute. Your so-called legal so-called guardian has left you in the house on your own . . . ?

In ten seconds I'd be bundled off to the Grandparents Duncan, never to be returned to Lil. I could give them Jaz and Zelda's phone number, but I wasn't sure if I could trust them to be quick enough to cover Lil's absence for me. No, I couldn't, not after this morning on the phone with Jaz.

Another police station scenario grew in my mind as I trudged across the city. It went the same as before up to the bit about my address. Then the police officer would lean forward.

You live in Parkside? Why, then, catch a bus up Magill Road—the opposite direction almost?

Obviously I couldn't say it was because I saw my grandmother looking unreal and I tried to spy on her. A couple of seconds would tick by before I could say I caught the wrong bus by mistake, and it'd sound like a lie.

But they'd pretend to believe me.

So you found yourself up at the top of Magill Road with no bus fare or ticket. So you robbed the bus driver to get money to get home?

Or they'd disbelieve me at once.

You know this guy wearing the ski mask, don't you. You had it planned between you. But you had to play the innocent and find a police station because the bus driver's going to be able to identify you, isn't he? Limpy. Freckleface.

No. No. I swear. Let me phone a lawyer . . .

You're too young for lawyers. Come along to the fingerprint machine. We'll phone your parents to get them here.

I don't live with my parents . . . Conversation as before.

I was drooping with hunger, dopey from the bang on my head, and these police station scenes had as much reality as the bus holdup. I kept walking, faster now, starting to half believe I'd escaped the police while they weren't looking.

And I was hearing so clearly Lil asking that same question. *What were you doing on a bus to Magill?* She wouldn't believe for a moment I made a mistake with the bus.

I saw you dressed up like a model, Lil, so I followed you and that guy to spy on you.

Impossible. I could never let her know that.

The Birthday Present

I woke in a hurry the next morning, thinking the telephone was ringing. I was dreaming the sound. As I propped myself on my elbow and raised my head, the pillow came too. Without thinking I pushed it away, and then watched in horror as drops of fresh red blood fell onto the blue pillowcase. There were darker bloodstains from where I'd irritated the graze on my face during the night.

I'd arrived home too tired to eat, too tired to wash or even look at the damage in the mirror.

ST was throwing herself against the bedroom door. She hadn't been fed either. I put on a droopy robe that used to belong to Pat, dark red terry cloth. I went into the bathroom and turned on the shower as hot as I could bear, and stood under it for so long that it cooled as the hot water supply ran out. The freshness of the cool water made my skin tingle.

I wiped the steam from the mirror so I could see the bleeding bit on my face. It was just a scratch, one only, from my forehead across the temple. It had stopped bleeding. It wouldn't need stitches. All the same, it would still be show-ing when Lil got back. Accident at the gym? I thought that place was supposed to make you fit, she'd say, not knock you about. It was possible she'd visit the gym, make a complaint. He wasn't even here that night, they'd say.

There was not only my face to worry about, there was my missing gym gear and all that had happened last night. If I was going to the police, I couldn't leave it much longer. Maybe I could say some kid stole my gear while I was out-side the railroad station. But then the bus driver could still identify me.

Too hard. I put bacon on the skillet, bread in the toaster, and gave ST some cold chicken and old roast pumpkin; then turned on the radio to help me put off thinking about mak-ing decisions.

It was the nine o'clock news. Bombs exploding in central London. An Australian tourist lost in Nepal. A successful giraffe birth at the Adelaide Zoo. Then: "Police are still look-ing for two people involved in the armed holdup of a met-ropolitan bus early last evening. One is described as a man around thirty years old, heavy build. The other is a youth in his teens, tall, thin, long sandy hair, pronounced limp."

It was as bad as I'd feared. The bus driver believed I was part of the holdup.

My life was getting horribly unreal. I wished Lil were here.

But Lil's life suddenly had unreality too, my knowledge of it, anyway. She didn't keep clothes like that here. She must keep them somewhere else, wherever it was that she became someone different. She had a whole other life apart from her one with me.

But then it could be that she'd had a meeting with a famous TV producer. One of her soap opera ideas had been bought by a television company. She was finalizing the deal so she could spring it on me as a big surprise. Or, maybe she had a secret life with that man. I'd never thought that Lil might have a love affair. I liked the TV scenario better, but I was afraid that the second was more likely.

I wished she were here. I couldn't decide what to do about the bus holdup. Wrong: I'd decided. Definitely I wanted to stay away from the police. I suspected that this was a wrong decision and the longer I left it the more difficult it would be.

Lie low, and hope it will all go away, I told myself. Gideon joined in. "Never go to the police. Even if they haven't got anything on you, they'll find something."

He spoke cynically, almost bitterly, as if from his own experience. I wasn't sure about that yet. However, other things were becoming clearer about Gideon's life. I took my bacon sandwich through to my room. I threw the blood-stained pillow into the hallway, and closed the door.

Gideon's mother and father ran a deli on Port Road. Rather like the one ST ran into on the night of the—that night. Very much like that deli. Maybe the same one.

Over the last few years business had grown worse and worse. Gideon's parents used to employ a series of college students to help with the sandwich-making, cleaning, stocking the shelves, and serving the customers. But the customers grew fewer and spent less money, and Gideon's parents had to fire the current student. They kept the deli open longer hours.

For a while Gideon's older sister Angela worked in the deli, but then she suddenly—more with relief to be getting away than for real love, Gideon suspected—married one of her boyfriends and moved to Sydney.

Gideon's mother worked more hours to help his father. One or both of them were at the deli from six in the morning until nine thirty at night.

Gideon offered to help at the deli after school and on weekends. No, they said. You are a clever boy. Your job is to study, learn a lot, read everything, play sports with your friends, keep fit and healthy. There were also the unspoken words. We let your sister work there and look what happened. She left us.

But Gideon knew that Angela hadn't had much choice. It was work in the deli or no job at all once she left school. Gideon's parents expected him to have a different future, but he wasn't sure if they had much of a grip on the real world.

And he badly needed some money. On the morning of his fifteenth birthday, alone in the apartment before school as usual, Gideon rolled a skinny joint with the scrappy remains in the matchbox. "This is your last free ride," Tony Bliss had said.

Gideon had felt annoyed about that. He'd thought there was an unspoken deal between them that Gideon supplied Tony Bliss with information for homework assignments and slid him answers in tests, in return for a matchboxful every couple of weeks. Anyway, Gideon knew that Tony Bliss got as much dope as he wanted from his uncle who had a plantation among his sweetcorn and sunflowers and windbreak poplars in the hills.

"Last free ride?" Gideon had said. "So you're going to do your own homework now?"

"Nah. I'm finished with school. Got to make a living from now on. So, no more freebies."

Gideon wondered if he'd get something salable from his parents for his birthday.

After school Angela phoned to wish him many happy returns: "Someone in this family better be happy." She obviously wasn't. She and Steve were both on unemployment and sick of it. She told Gideon she thought she was pregnant and Steve was ticked off about that. "Don't tell Mom," she said.

After Angela hung up, Gideon thought about her being pregnant, about becoming Uncle Gideon, and wished Angela could be happier about it. Then he thought some more about money.

At five thirty his father arrived home. The late afternoon rush hour used to be the busiest time at the deli apart from lunch, but a few weeks ago the Department of Transportation had put NO PARKING 4–6 PM signs along the road outside, so there was nowhere to stop the car, dash in for milk or frozen peas or salami.

His father carried two packages wrapped in green-and-white paper, and a six-pack of light beer. He handed the packages to Gideon, and one of the cans. It wasn't that cold. "Your mother and I wanted to take you out for dinner for your birthday," he said. "But it'd be after nine thirty. Well, too late for a school night."

Gideon fetched two glasses from the drainer by the sink, delaying by polishing them on a dish towel. He dreaded opening the presents. His father poured the beers. One of the parcels was obviously a book, a paperback, flat and slightly flexible. The other was smaller, a hard oblong. He opened that one first.

It was a plastic case holding a fountain pen. Gideon said *wow* as he unscrewed the top. The pen had a broad silver nib. He opened the other parcel. *A Beginner's Guide to Calligraphy*. Inside were examples of careful alphabets, capital letters embellished with flourishes, phrases like "Presented in Recognition of Fifty Years' Faithful Service" with blank lines underneath to practice copying. The back cover of the book was creased and had a couple of staple marks; the plastic box for the pen was scratched. Gideon knew they were sales samples from a failed venture to introduce some diversity into the stock at the deli. For Gideon's purposes, they were about as salable as old newspapers.

He could tell his father was watching his face, waiting for a response. Gideon made a smile, widened his eyes to show excitement, and embraced his father.

"Your mother and I thought it would stand you in good stead, a skill like this. Look good on exam papers and what have you. It impresses people, you know, a good hand."

It was always the pattern, Gideon realized. His father knew it was a ratshit present, a cop-out, but forced Gideon to play a grateful game or feel guilty. Feel guilty anyway.

Why couldn't there be some honesty? Why didn't his father say there's not a spare dollar in our lives just now for presents. Here's some samples from the shop. If you don't find them useful, well no big deal. Instead he sat there looking as eager for gratitude as if he'd given Gideon a computer. And Gideon played the game. ("That's great, Dad. I need any advantage I can get at exams. Thanks a lot.") But he knew things had changed. He'd recognized the guilt game.

His father finished his beer and went back to work. Gideon drank another can, then another. He was thinking about offering Tony Bliss a business proposition.

Gideon's story faded. I was tired. I could tell there was something familiar about Gideon's relationship with his father, something that reminded me of Pat's stories about the family he grew up with, the family who adopted him when he was a baby. It was intriguing. But there was no more time—ST was barking at the end of the hallway and there was someone at the door. The combined noise penetrated my thinking space.

Through the knobbly green-and-red glass panes I could see that the Grandparents Duncan were here.

The Grandparents Duncan

"Ian, darling." Grandmother Duncan was through the door and into the living room before I said anything. Grandfather Duncan was still at their car. All I could see of him was his wide trousered backside as he heaved something out of the trunk. I held the door open while he staggered in with a cardboard box labeled "Great Western Brut Champagne." Some muddy green leaves nodded through the top of the box.

"Take them straight out back," Grandmother Duncan instructed him. "The cuttings for Lilian," she told me, unnecessarily. "We'll leave the box too, if you don't mind. We seem to have millions. The wretched local supermarket has jumped onto the recycling bandwagon and we don't get those useful plastic bags anymore." She stopped, her eyes looking everywhere around the living room, the divider bench, the kitchen area beyond. "Oh, dear," she said softly.

The pizza box lay open on the carpet near the sofa

where I'd left it to share with ST—when? The first night Lil was away. The kitchen benches, the divider, the stove were all loaded with stuff like the fatty skillet, stray bacon rinds, eggshells, burnt toast, the chicken carcass, butter, cups, glasses, knives. I was amazed. How had all that happened?

Grandmother Duncan chuckled. "You put the kettle on for coffee, darling, and I'll get cracking on cleaning up this lot. How like a boy. Housework's a dirty word, isn't it?"

How like a boy. I resented that. Lil and I shared a passion, maybe an obsession, for order and clear spaces. She said that orderly surroundings allowed for interesting chaos in the mind. Housework wasn't an issue between us, not even a word we used. So I couldn't account for this disorder, apart from a certain pressure, an amount of preoccupation, in the last couple of days.

Grandfather Duncan had placed the box of cuttings near the end of the brick walk. He came back in the kitchen door, puffing, rubbing his hands together. "Damn heavy," he said.

"Wipe your feet!" said Grandmother Duncan. "And watch your tongue."

Grandfather Duncan wiped his feet for a long time. He gave me a wink as he passed his wife, and then sat heavily on a sofa in the living room. At his side were the photos of Pat, Elaine, Lil, me, some still lying loose on the carpet. Clearly I hadn't finished putting them away yesterday.

"The box is heavy," Grandmother Duncan was saying from the kitchen, "because I put lots of good earth in with the cuttings. So Lilian won't have to do much digging. They'd look quite good in terra-cotta pots, darling, if you've got any lying around."

I was watching Grandfather Duncan turning over the

pages of one of the photo albums, hesitating at the early ones of his daughter Elaine both with me as a bulge and me as a baby. I wondered what he was thinking. He never said much. It was always Grandmother Duncan doing the talking, the bossing, pulling the strings.

He paused over a photo of Elaine embracing Pat, both wearing huge smiles, another of the early photos. He spent a long time looking at it, a hint of a smile on his face. "God," he said at last, "that Pat was a feckless bugger. Couldn't keep two cents in his pocket."

"The day I disconnected my grandmother's brake cable," I heard Gideon say, "I made sure my grandfather was in the car too. They both went over the cliff."

Good idea. Suddenly I had nothing to say to my grandfather, didn't want to be in the same room. I wished the Duncans would disappear.

Pat had never kept it a secret that he couldn't stand Grandmother Duncan, but he seemed to get along well with Grandfather. They'd be chatting and chortling out in the garden while Lil sat there, looking strained, coping with Grandmother Duncan's monologues. And now all Grandfather Duncan could find to say about Pat was that he was a feckless bugger.

Grandmother Duncan came in with three mugs of coffee on a tray. "I couldn't find the cups and saucers," she said. "I'm sure Lilian does have some."

"We always use mugs," I said.

"Oh, yes, but surely not for guests."

I took the tray from her and put it on the coffee table by the sofa. "Your limp seems a lot better, darling," she said. Then she gave a little shriek and put her fingers toward the cut on my face. "Whatever happened?"

"Nothing . . . nothing . . . just a collision at the gym."

"You poor baby. Did your aunt put some disinfectant on it?"

It took me a second or two to realize she meant Zelda. She still believed, despite all the mess here, that I was actually staying at Jaz's. "We went to your aunt's before we came here. That cold little miss—Jasmine isn't it?—said you were here for the day working on a school project."

It seemed that Jaz had covered for me—not actually lied, but made it sound as if I was staying with them and coming back here during the daytime. I was surprised. After the way Jaz had spoken on the phone, I thought she'd have jumped at the chance to squeal on me to the Grandparents Duncan.

I glanced at the clock on the VCR—two forty-five already. I'd been oblivious of the hours passing, shut in my room, engrossed with the keyboard. Right now Gideon and his life seemed very far away. Gideon would never let himself be trapped into a dreary tea party like this.

Nor would Pat. He'd have found some excuse to go off somewhere. I decided that Pat had only pretended to like Grandfather Duncan. I always knew Pat was fascinated by his work, and used to ask searching questions about it that Grandmother Duncan found *distasteful*: "So what happens if you forget to put them in the fridge?" Before he retired, Grandfather Duncan was a funeral director. "Everyone must be dying to meet him," Pat would say, digging me in the ribs.

"We must be off, darling," Grandmother Duncan was saying. She collected the mugs and carried them into the kitchen. I heard her gasp. "Oh, that wretched dog!" There was a rapid rat-tat-tat on the windowpane.

I looked out. There was ST, back arched, concentrating furiously, balanced on the box of cuttings and dropping a glossy brown turd.

"It's all right," I said to Grandmother Duncan, "she

does real firm ones. I'll be able to shift it easily."

In a moment or two Grandmother Duncan seemed to recover. There was more talk about getting Lil to phone her, and I must take care and look after myself, a peck on the cheek and they were gone.

Pat's Childhood

I watched them through the front windows, laughing at Grandmother Duncan's waving arms and alarmed face as Grandfather nearly backed into a dark blue car that was pulling into the curb.

They were gone finally. Alone again. No, not alone.

"You should have asked him if he's lost any more corpses recently," Gideon said.

That made me laugh again. Pat's favorite story—Grandfather Duncan and the missing body.

The phone rang. Gideon left. "Hello?"

"Skillington here. School librarian."

The Skull! "Yes?" I said cautiously.

"I expect you'll be relieved to know that the library book you borrowed before the end of the term has been found. I'm told you can collect it from the lost property office at the Central Police Station. See that you do." And he hung up.

That was the paperback in my gym bag. It had the school's name on it.

"It's a trap," said Gideon.

Not necessarily. The gunman probably chucked it out of the bag. Anyone could have found it in a gutter somewhere and handed it in to the lost property office.

"Think about it. It's school break. Nobody at the police station's going to chase around finding the school librarian's home phone number over a ten-dollar paperback. Unless . . ."

Gideon was right. I started to feel uneasy. The Skull must have a home to go to, even if it was hard to picture him anywhere other than hooked up to the library computer.

". . . unless the book is a direct link to the bus holdup."

It wasn't likely that the Skull would remember me personally or my connection with that particular book. It was true that I'd gone into the library every day for two weeks asking for it when I knew my name was next on the list. But each time I'd had to tell him my name again, and he never lifted his eyes in their hollow ashy-gray sockets from the computer screen, so I was sure he'd have no idea what I looked like.

"So the cops made him go to the school, crank up the computer, find your name. Then they made him help trap you by phoning. They've probably got your fingerprints off the book."

Fingerprints?

"They'll be able to prove you were on that bus. They'll find your prints there."

Could they? Maybe, on a steel railing or something, but they'd find a million others too.

"Doesn't matter. Even if they can't find your prints, they'll fix it up so they're there."

Again here was Gideon speaking with authority about cops, as if he had personal knowledge. I slid into Gideon's life, glad to avoid thinking about my own.

I caught a glimpse of his parents, heartbroken, shocked, in a courtroom, watching Gideon in the dock. Or maybe before then, at the police station, handing over bail money to release their son from the holding cells. Where would they have raised the bail money?

Gideon's parents don't rage at him on the way home. They're quiet, sort of embarrassed, almost as if they're the ones who committed the crime. Gideon is the one with the bravado, the rage. His father drives; his mother is hunched miserably in the back seat. She wears the speckled gray dress that matches her hair and she's almost invisible. Before they're halfway home Gideon jumps out of the car at a traffic light and flings the door shut behind him. His father calls out to him, but then the light changes and he drives on, looking troubled.

I knew what was happening to these people, Gideon's parents. They were being shaped in a devious way by my memories—mainly secondhand—of the couple who had adopted Pat as a baby. I had met them only once.

Their name was O'Leary and they gave my father the name Patrick. When Pat left school and came to live with Lil, sometimes he called himself Pat O'Leary and sometimes Pat Ganty. By the time he got a passport and took off with Elaine on the flight that didn't last the distance, he was Pat Ganty. Elaine was always Elaine Duncan, even after they married.

Gideon's father was now much less like the harassed man I'd seen in the deli shouting at ST, and more like mild, quiet Mr. O'Leary. Other things were different, though. The O'Learys had plenty of money, and gave Pat expensive presents every birthday and Christmas while he was growing up. He told me about them. Things like full-sized drum sets, stereos, and the best sports gear.

The O'Learys never hit Pat or shouted at him or punished him. "Not that I ever did anything wrong, really," Pat told me. "Not when I was little, anyway. I didn't dare. It was like I'd break their hearts or something."

Pat told me some of this stuff the day he and I drove up to Hahndorf, the day the car ran off the road and I got my peculiar knee. Other stuff he told me later, and some I heard from Lil, but by now it all ran together in a continuous stream of Pat's voice in my head. There was one story that definitely was part of the Hahndorf trip.

"When I was about nine," he told me, "a kid in my class at school turned up with a huge bruise on his face and great red welts on his legs. He said to us—not to the teacher, of course—that his father had bashed him for calling him a fuckwit. I really liked that joining-up of words. I kept on saying it inside my head. When I got home, I opened the bottom drawer under the bench in the kitchen, and lifted the shiny paper stuff they had in there to line the drawer, and wrote FUCKWITS! in fat black felt tip on the painted wood.

"Of course nothing happened. Days passed and I got worried. I hated going into the kitchen because I couldn't stop staring at the drawer as if the word was going to start bleeding through the wood or something. One day I tried to wash it off. Couldn't, of course. The next day after school Dad was home from work, looking at me reproachfully. Mom was in bed with the door closed and I didn't see her for three days. As soon as I could I checked the drawer. The word was gone completely. Fresh white paint, new shiny paper. And neither of them ever, ever said anything about it."

On that Hahndorf trip, Pat had driven back to Adelaide a different way from the freeway so we could look at the view from the Norton Summit pub. We stayed at the pub for a couple of hours. I had the feeling that Pat was putting off going home. I was old enough to know you can't drink that many whiskeys and then drive fast down a winding road in an old car with unreliable brakes, but not old enough, or not assertive enough, or maybe I loved Pat too much, to lie on the road, scream and have a tantrum, refuse to get in the car. I could have saved him, and I didn't.

At the sharpest hairpin bend, it seemed Pat didn't even try to pull the steering wheel. The car shot up the bank, hung in the air, then tumbled back onto its roof and over. Somehow my knee got jammed in the passenger door that had popped slightly open, then crushed when the car rolled.

So I was in the hospital forever, it felt like, and the O'Learys arrived from Brisbane because Pat had a broken pelvis and was in the hospital too. It was during those endless days—bored with daytime television, unable to concentrate on schoolwork—that I started reading properly.

Mrs. O'Leary was interested in the pile of novels I'd gotten from the hospital library. I told her the plots of the ones I'd read and she asked me what I liked about them. She went out for a while. Mr. O'Leary talked to me about sports and said that with some good physiotherapy I'd be as good on the field as ever—and it was he, I realized, who had first suggested rowing, which became my favorite sport.

Mrs. O'Leary came back with three Robert Cormier books for me. Then they went away.

"They were really nice," I'd said accusingly to Pat.

He held up his hands, laughing. "Hang on. Did I ever say they weren't? Lovely people. Gave me everything I wanted. I wasn't some sort of *victim*. It wasn't their fault I was a disappointment." He was still smiling, but I could pick up an undercurrent of meaning in his words.

Sometime later he said to me, almost casually, "There are people like that, Ian. They're endlessly mild and self-effacing. They terrorize you with their meekness. You feel sorry for them and they always, always get their own way. You feel guilty if you don't give in."

So. This was how I was starting to see Gideon's parents. I hadn't intended that Gideon or anyone associated with him would resemble even small pieces of people I actually knew. But maybe this was okay. The O'Learys were people I knew only a little bit. When Pat left school and came to live with Lil and Elaine, who was pregnant with me, they'd sold everything and moved to Brisbane.

Back to Wednesday. I was kneeling on the floor tidying the photographs Grandfather Duncan had disorganized, and stacking them back into the drawer. Gideon was hissing in my ear about the cops. I was overwhelmed with a need for Lil to be here to take charge. She could say something like: "It's simple, Ian. Someone helpful at the lost property office called the school library and Mr. Skillington happened to be there. You know he often works after hours."

But now I wasn't sure that I knew her as well as I thought I did. She might tell me to sort out my problems myself. And to mind my own business about the casino.

All the same, that early evening when I heard a movement on the veranda and ST's welcoming bark, I was still desperately hoping it was Lil, home early.

The Killing

"Hi. Our Wednesday night date—remember?"
It was Jaz, holding a casserole dish covered with aluminum foil. She handed me the dish, picked up ST and walked past me into the living room. "I made lasagna. We just have to heat it up. It took hours and I used every pot in the kitchen so you'd better like it." By now she was on the sofa, ST foaming about on her knees. "God, it's good to get away from Zelda for a bit. She's started tai chi and she's always standing around with her knees bent and a constipated look on her face. You don't have to keep on holding that dish, Ian. Why not shove it in the oven? You're very quiet. Stunned, even. You had forgotten about our date, betcha."

That was true, but I was also thinking that Jaz was herself again, back to normal, not the interfering judgmental pseudo grown-up she'd been on the phone. And back-to-normal Jaz, my good friend and ally, might have some useful ideas about my various problems.

I turned on the oven, waited till the flame showed through the little round window at the back, turned the dial back to 350 degrees. "With or without the foil?"

"Leave it on for a while. Ten minutes or so."

"Do you want something to drink?"

"Coffee. Between, you know?"

I knew. Lil made very strong coffee, I made it weak. Jaz liked it medium. Slowly Jaz was making life less desperate, bringing normality by using familiar codes.

"That's a huge pile of lasagna," I said, standing by the bench, deciding how much coffee to use.

"Yes, well, Zelda thinks Lil's here so she said not to halve the recipe. You know how Lil eats."

"You told Zelda that Lil's here?"

"I didn't tell her. She just assumed. You don't think Zelda would let you stay here on your own, do you?"

Definitely Jaz could be trusted with my secrets. The kettle was boiling. I sloshed water on the coffee. Then I heard Jaz's next words from the living room. "Anyway, I think it's illegal to leave kids on their own in houses overnight. So you better not do anything dumb like burning the place down, or I'll be in the shit too for covering for you."

Kids. Dumb. I felt cold. In a couple of sentences Jaz had lost about a million points.

I walked back into the living room and then saw that Jaz wasn't alone. Gideon was on the sofa beside her.

He was sitting close, almost crowding her. He smelled an apple scent of shampoo. She looked puzzled, frowning a little. His arm was along the sofa back behind her, and slowly it dropped to encircle her shoulders. She inched away. "What's going on?" Still puzzled, not angry yet. His other hand brushed her knee, then settled there.

"Look, don't be a complete *dickhead*." Now she tried to stand up, but Gideon's hold on her was stronger than she realized and he pulled her toward him with sudden sexual urgency. With a fast jab of her elbows on the back of the sofa she was free, standing over him, breathing hard, her eyes fierce. "What the hell do you think you're doing?"

Gideon shrugged. "What's the matter? Trying to pretend you don't go for that sort of thing?"

She didn't answer, just narrowed her eyes. She was calmer now. Cold and angry.

"Or maybe," Gideon's voice was lower, "maybe it's girls you like better. That's the truth of it, isn't it?"

Her voice was pure hate. "Maybe I do. So keep out of my way. If you dare touch me again, I'll get you for attempted rape. I don't ever want to see your slime face again, Ian Ganty. Keep out of my range from now on."

She was gone. The front door slammed. *Ian Ganty*. She blamed me. She thought it was me. You *bastard*, Gideon.

I leaned forward so my head was on my knees, wrapping my arms around my legs, trying to stop shaking. I was terrified. Gideon was invading me.

But he wasn't real. I'd made him up. All I needed to do was unmake him.

"Inventing me was the easy part," said Gideon. "The hard part will be getting rid of me."

Oh, really? I stood up and walked to my room, each step firm and purposeful. I looked at my face in the mirror on the wall beside the window. My face, lips pressed together hard, light blue eyes, fine straight fair hair, long, needing a wash. The shaded blue of the wall behind me matched exactly the shading on each side of the mirror, so if I blurred my eyes slightly, the mirror had no edges and my face looked as if it was projected onto the wall itself. As I squinted, there for an instant on the wall was *Gideon's* face, not mine. I blinked hard, feeling the shakes again. I told my face, "Remember what you're here to do, Ian Ganty."

I switched on the word processor, drumming my fingers while it whirred and lumbered along, taking its time to bring up the files. I clicked through to GIDEON.DOC and hit the delete button. CONFIRM DELETE. Y. Gone.

I got out my English folder and found the notes from class last Friday.

HOLIDAY ASSIGNMENT: INVENT A CHARACTER.
    GIVE HIM/HER:
—*name*
—*appearance*
—*setting: living space (town/country?), time (past?*
    present? future?)
—*background (family, friends)*
—*psychology (likes, dislikes, tendencies, passions, moods)*
ONLY TWO RULES:
(a) must be human
(b) must be invented

This was in my handwriting, copied from Ms. Blaine's instructions on the board.

Underneath I'd written (right then, still in class while everyone else was talking about holidays and dates and packing their books into bags and clattering chairs and desks): *Gideon. 17 or 18. Dark hair. Wears black. Moves like a cat. Doesn't give a stuff about anyone else.*

I tore this page of notes into smaller and smaller pieces.

I looked at the scraps of paper on the desk for a while, then decided to take them to the fireplace and burn them. Tearing up the page had been satisfying, but it didn't seem enough. Gideon was still around.

I wished that I'd printed out the notes on the word processor file before deleting them, so I could have burned them too. The screen was glowing. Of course. The file was still there, transferred to the hard disc, held until the word processor was switched off. That was why he wasn't quite gone.

I looked through the list of hard disc files. There it was: GIDEON.LIM. I hit PRINT. More creaks and then a whir from the printer.

This was taking ages. The printer was going even more slowly than usual. I had an image of Gideon resisting, refusing to be squeezed out into those little dots on the paper. I read some of the lines as the printer head crawled across the page.

Older sister Angela. Married. Gone to Sydney.

Parents broke. Business going down tube. Anxious. Ineffectual.

School. Gideon leaves 15? 16? Has to leave. Caught dealing in dope?

Maybe leaves anyway, schools useless no jobs. A better living to be made dealing.

There was more of it, pages and pages, sometimes complete sentences and paragraphs, direct speech. I had no idea I'd written so much. As the printer ground on, I began to worry that there would be no end, that Gideon was creating more and more detail about himself, that it would go on minute by minute as he lived and breathed as if he *were* a living, breathing, real human entity.

But no. The printer stopped. I tore off the last page.

She's inviting him, Gideon knows this. She's curled on the end of the sofa, leaning her head back, rumpling her hair with her fingers so he can see the curve and movement of her breasts and smell the green apple scent of the shampoo she uses.

That was where it ended. My heart was thumping and my fingers had started their shakes again so I had trouble folding the pages together and I didn't have the strength to tear them. Just burn them, I told myself, looking again at my reflection—checking. Crumple them and burn them.

Matches from the kitchen, into the living room, move the screen from the fireplace. All the time, Gideon's voice. "You've been thinking that way about Jaz for quite a while now, haven't you? You suspected she was gay and that made her even more exotic and desirable. Right?" The pages didn't want to burn. I had to do it page by page, using a lot of matches. I could still read words on the black fragments so I smashed them up with the poker, pulverizing them to drifts of ash and then nothing.

Gone. The house was silent. I breathed deeply several times, consciously relaxing my shoulders. Tomorrow Lil would be back. Everything would be safe and normal again. Gideon was no more.

I heard his mocking voice. "Oh, really?"

Go back to my room. Turn off the word processor.

Part Two

About Not
Giving a Stuff

I killed Gideon. I didn't know whether to be glad or not. He'd been great at first: strong, lithe, adventurous, daring; I'd built him carefully brick by brick. But it was as if I'd made this brick building from the inside and forgotten to leave a door. The only way I could get out was to smash it down.

As I turned off the word processor that Wednesday night, and thought that the last trace of Gideon was wiped out, I decided I was glad. I used to like him, and I envied his street-smartness, but in the end he wasn't on my side anymore. And he was basically a crook.

Not that crooks were strangers to our family. And here I introduce the last grandparent needed to complete the set: Pat's real father—that is, Lil's partner in my father's conception. There wasn't any mystery about him. It was just that he was in Pentridge Gaol in Melbourne, and as far as Lil was concerned he didn't rate any mention.

A few years ago I'd been fascinated by him and what he'd

done, and I asked Lil endless questions, but then other things happened and he'd dropped out of my mind.

Dan Kinnard, my father's real father, was arrested for drug dealing. There was an intricate network of dealers and suppliers and collectors, rather like a pyramid, with one man at the peak. The pyramid was dismantled and the details were printed in the papers, and I read it all eagerly. Dan Kinnard was accused of being the man at the peak: the mastermind.

Pat had known that his real father's name was Daniel Kinnard, but Lil had told him that she had no idea where in the world he was and no interest in finding out. She also said that Dan didn't know that Pat existed.

And then, the front-page headlines over four years ago.

ARREST: DRUG RING LEADER
Victorian police are confident of a successful conclusion to their two-year investigation into Victorian drug distribution with the arrest of 50-year-old Daniel Kerry Kinnard (pictured left). Kinnard is alleged to control a network which may eventually reach users as young as ten years old . . .

I saw it first, because I'd gone to the corner deli to get milk for breakfast and the paper. There were a couple of people at the counter before me, so I read the headlines, looked at the photo. "Wow!" I shouted.

"Good news?" said the woman at the deli, smiling as I paid her.

"That's my grandfather!" I waved the paper with its huge headlines and the photo of a man in profile taken through the back window of a police car.

I ran the two blocks home, ST barking all the way. "Look at this!" I shouted as I rushed into the living room. Lil was at the dining table drinking black coffee. Pat was on the sofa lighting a cigarette. Elaine was in the kitchen buttering toast. They all came and leaned over the paper I'd spread on the table.

Nobody said anything for a long time. "Well, it's him, isn't it?" I asked, looking at their faces. Lil's was expressionless. Elaine's was upset, and I could see her eyes reading the text rapidly. Pat was looking at the photo. Still none of them said a word.

Lil appeared to lose interest. She sat back and went on with her coffee. Elaine got to "continued page 2" and picked up the paper to turn the page. "You don't seem very surprised," she said to Lil a bit suspiciously, as if she thought Lil had known all along that Dan was a drug pusher.

Elaine was halfway through page two before Lil answered. "I'm horrified, but not surprised. Dan never did give a stuff about anyone else."

Lil was now watching Pat, whose eyes were fixed on the page-two photo of Dan, walking between two policemen, holding a newspaper up so his face was half covered. You could still see his heavy dark-rimmed glasses, his balding head. The previous photo had shown his medium-sized mustache.

"Well, for God's sake, don't let's tell Mom and Dad." Elaine meant her parents, the Grandparents Duncan.

"If it's any comfort to you, Elaine, no one's ever known of any connection between Daniel Kinnard and me, and there's no reason why anyone ever should."

I remembered the scene in the deli. Mrs. Bennedotti, the deli owner; a couple of kids coming in the door, talking, not taking any notice; and, oh, no, Mr. Davidson, who lived across the street in the impressive two-story house and who employed a gardener. I knew that Grandmother Duncan belonged to the same bridge club as Mrs. Davidson. Pat and Elaine and Lil knew it too because Grandmother Duncan mentioned it often. I wanted to die.

"Uh, oh," I said in the doleful way that's supposed to make people laugh and put them in a good mood before you drop the bad news. "I said in the deli he was my grandfather. To Mrs. Bennedotti. Mr. Davidson was buying a paper, too."

Elaine looked appalled. "That was really, full-on, *thick*," she said.

"Well, I didn't think about what he's supposed to have done. I was just excited to see the name, and the picture and everything."

"That's right, you didn't think," Elaine said. "You never do."

That was unfair. I was always thinking. I thought about things and people all the time. My mother was angry, getting ready to say more to me, but Lil intervened. "Don't let's get upset, Elaine. We'll just have to wear it. And anyway, he might not say anything to Mrs. Davidson. You know they never talk to each other."

It was true. Mr. Davidson lived upstairs, Mrs. Davidson downstairs. They employed two housekeepers, one each, who came on different days.

My mother took a deep breath, then said to me, "Shouldn't you be getting your things ready for school?" I went into the kitchen and collected some fruit and granola bars for lunch, moving stealthily, waiting for the next words. I heard Elaine speaking in a low voice. "He's my son. Would you not keep interfering when I'm talking to him."

Lil said in a mild way, "I'm sorry, Elaine."

Pat had been silent through all this. Now I heard him say, "Well, it looks like I'm going to be bald sooner or later."

"Of course you're not," Lil said. "You're not like him in any way, not to the slightest degree."

Elaine came into the kitchen. I knew she knew I was listening. "You mustn't say anything about this at school," she said. "You do understand that, Ian, don't you?" She put her arms around me and I felt her puffing warm breath on the top of my head as she'd done every now and then ever since I could remember. My hair was so fine, she used to say, it blew around like thistledown. "Sorry I said you were thick," she murmured.

"I won't say anything at school. I'm really sorry, Mom."

She stood back. "That's all right, my darling. See you later, then."

A few months later Daniel Kinnard's court case started, and there was information in the newspaper every day, and more photos. We bought the Melbourne *Age*, too, which had even more coverage. Pat and I read every word. Elaine was tight-lipped and uninterested. Of course the Grandparents Duncan had found out through the bridge club, all of whose members knew that Grandmother Duncan's daughter had married into a drug ring. Her mother was mortified, Elaine said.

The court case dragged on. By the time it finished and Dan was sentenced to seven years in Pentridge, a number of other things had happened. Our car crash, for instance, and the surprise visit of the O'Learys, and Pat's own court case, where he lost his driver's license for two years for drunk driving.

One morning the paper said that Daniel Kinnard's lawyers were starting an appeal against the length of the sentence. Pat said, "Maybe I'd like to meet him. You know, say who I am."

Elaine's face went white. Pat continued, talking idly, turning to the World News section, "I could visit him in Pentridge. They're allowed visitors, aren't they?"

After a moment, Lil said, "Not just anyone. You can't turn up like the visiting hours at the hospital."

"Well, I could write first." Pat seemed to be reading on, as if he had little real interest in what he was saying.

"Although it'd look a bit strange. He might think I'm some sort of crank. But you could write to him for me, Lil."

Lil didn't reply. Everyone was silent, almost not breathing.

"Telling him about me. Say I want to meet him."

At last Lil spoke. "I can't do that, Pat. I'm sorry, but I won't."

"Oh, well." Pat shrugged slightly as if to say forget it, and Elaine's face relaxed, and that was the end of it.

In the next few weeks more things happened. Elaine had her master's degree by then. An amazing letter arrived from California offering her a research position at an institution there, a one-year contract renewable to three, moving expenses for her family, a house on campus. It was a dream of an offer, Elaine said over and over.

Pat was ecstatic. "*California*," he kept repeating.

Before I knew it, they weren't discussing whether or not she'd accept the offer, but whether it would be better for me to have my next knee operation in a U.S. hospital or here. In other words, whether I'd go with them now, or follow later.

Then that discussion was dropped for a while, and Pat went back to saying "California" in a dazed voice, and Elaine continued wondering aloud who had been so impressed with her thesis that they'd sent it to that institution so *they'd* been so impressed they'd offered her a job.

I was confused. To live in the States—in California—for a year, or maybe three, sounded spectacular. But I couldn't even walk. Every day I had to have hideous and painful things done to my knee by a visiting nurse, and when that bit of bone mended, they were going to pull it all apart again and do the next bit.

I kept waiting for Lil to say something decisive, but she was staying right out of it. Already she suspected something that later turned out to be true. Grandmother

Duncan was behind the whole thing. She had pulled strings, either through the bridge club or her university connections, and Elaine's offer was part of an exchange with a similar, newly qualified researcher coming from the United States to an institution in Australia.

Well, there was nothing really sinister in that, as Lil said to me later. It wasn't necessarily true that Grandmother Duncan had organized the California job to get Elaine and Pat away from Australia for any particular reason. Elaine was clever, and would do the job well, and it was good to have experience in different countries. These arranged exchanges happened all the time.

It also took Pat's mind completely off any notion of contacting his criminal father. Dan Kinnard was never mentioned again. Pat took no notice of his appeal trial. It was all decided: Elaine and Pat were going; I would stay with Lil and join them later.

Suddenly we were seeing them off. There wasn't any time for long good-byes; as it was, they nearly missed the plane. They flew to Hawaii for a three-day vacation, and the next flight was the one with the faulty door hinge. A hole appeared where the side of the plane should be, and within the blink of an eye my parents and others with them were sucked out of the plane and pulverized.

It was lucky I was doing schoolwork at home those days. I knew it would have been hard for the other kids to stop talking—because of my parents—about the bits of bodies they found in the engine casings, the patina of blood and brain on the skin of the plane.

I wasn't crazy enough—quite—back then to blame the Grandparents Duncan for the fault in the door on that particular flight. But I had to put the blame somewhere. I chose them as the villains.

Dressing Up

Lil believed that people should give a stuff about other people. But that Wednesday night, sitting by the fireplace with the ashes of Gideon, I was strongly into self-preservation.

I was icy with fear at the memory of the stolen car, its speed, the responsiveness of the accelerator. It had been really easy to go along with the game that it was Gideon's car, that Gideon was driving. Now I had to acknowledge that Gideon had never been anything more than words in my brain. I'd seen a car with keys in its ignition, and I'd jumped in and driven off. My fingerprints would be in that car.

At any moment the cops would come back, this time to get me. It was too hard to sit here and wait. I had to go out, somewhere, anywhere; instinctively I needed to hide among people in the city.

Money. I didn't have any. Perhaps there'd be some in Lil's room.

Lil's jackets and sweaters and shirts hung in groups in her wardrobe. The jacket pockets were empty. Not even a forgotten coin. The drawers in a chest beside the wardrobe held nothing but piles of socks, underwear, gloves. The table by the window was just as orderly. Some notebooks, a few letters held together with a paper clip, bills waiting in a folder to be paid, a wooden box where the spare keys and stamps were kept. Nothing, no cash, no secrets. And no flash going-to-casino clothes, either.

The possibility of asking Jaz for a loan didn't stay in my mind for more than a quarter-second. I couldn't bear to think about Jaz.

Then there were the Grandparents Duncan. No, it wasn't possible to ask them for money. I remembered their talking about going to Clare or somewhere for the night. And even if they weren't away, there'd be questions, and triumph that they'd been able to give me something that Lil couldn't. Lil would hate it.

I found I was reaching out to the wooden box again, opening its lid, hardly aware of, or acknowledging, the plan starting to form. I extracted the keys I wanted, two keys on a ring with a small label: *front door*. The Grandparents Duncan front door. The keys had been there since my grandparents' summer vacation, when I'd had the job of feeding their two cats twice a day, and watering their plants and the garden, and collecting the mail.

Grandmother Duncan had for months been building a model of Buckingham Palace out of two-dollar coins. She'd found the plan in a magazine. It took hundreds of coins to build all those walls and doorways. I decided that just a piece of the front stairs would be enough for me, and might not even be missed.

I dropped the keys back in the box and closed its lid with a crash. Crazy idea. Gideon would have done it like a shot, but I wasn't Gideon. I saw my reflection in the mirror on the wardrobe door. Definitely not Gideon.

A car drove up outside. It turned into the next-door driveway, reversed out, and then parked by the curb. I could see it through Lil's curtains—a dark-colored car with smoked windows. I was sure it was a plainclothes police car. I stood still, straining to hear if its engine was still running. Was this going to be it? Handcuffs, warnings about my rights? They wouldn't use handcuffs. I was too young.

The car moved on. I heard it slow down at the intersection, then accelerate away until I couldn't hear it anymore.

From the wardrobe I took a jacket of Lil's I liked, soft leather cut like a bomber jacket. It fit me quite well. It was a little like the one that Gideon had worn.

In the second drawer were Lil's leather driving gloves. They were a perfect fit. I knew that because they had been my birthday present to her in May, and our hands were the same size.

I took the keys labeled *front door* from the box. In the hallway I attached them to my keys and put them in the top pocket of the bomber jacket. I checked that ST was inside, and latched the cat-flap. Then I turned off all the lights, and shut the door behind me.

In the street I stepped quietly along the dark side of the sidewalk like a cat. Through the silent children's park, along the stormwater canal path, dodging the delicate fronds of the peppercorn trees. I didn't see anybody. Not even a dog barked.

Three more blocks through the quiet streets to the green-painted iron fence outside the Grandparents Duncan house. I could see lights showing, but I knew they left some on when they were away, because varying them had been part of my vacation job.

I walked along the curving pathway between the rose

bushes and up the steps to the front door, and hesitated with the keys in my hand. A low rumble of voices came from inside the house. Possibly it was the radio—another trick to confuse burglars—but what if they'd changed their minds, not gone to Clare after all? I wondered if I should knock first, just in case. What story could I tell them if they answered the door?

I heard a car driving along the street. I froze, not daring to turn around. I suspected it was that same cop car, following me. It cruised slowly past. Desperate to look like an innocent visitor, I knocked on the door.

The car was gone. Nobody came to the door. I unlocked it and went inside.

The voices came from a radio in the hallway. It was a talk show. I half-listened as I walked cautiously up the hallway, peering into each shadowy room.

"He would have worked for that car, just like anyone else."

"But isn't that the point that the youths were trying to make? It doesn't matter how willing you are to earn the wherewithal to buy a car—you're stymied if there's no jobs."

"*My* point is, if you'll give me a chance to put it, is that if I get carted off to the hospital and my doctor has to jump in his car quickly to get there to treat me, I want him to have a pretty good and reliable car that's going to get him there and not break down at the first traffic light. What do these hoodlums want? I'd like to see them groaning in agony while their doctor waits at the bus stop or pumps up his bike tires."

"Good point, yes, thank you, caller. Now we have Pamela from Payneham. Good evening, Pamela."

"Very good evening to you. I think we need some compassion here. There are thousands of people out there at the point of desperation and no prospects of any improvement. That sort of desperation can lead to some pretty irrational acts. The problem . . ."

"Well, I think we can understand a couple of youths demanding the cash from the driver's wallet. But then to produce a can of gasoline and soak the car, throw a match at it and say that would teach him a lesson for being rich—I think we've got to agree that's going beyond irrationality."

"But don't you see it's symptomatic of the widening gap between the haves and the have-nots? You could almost say the youths acted entirely rationally. Their act was a symbolic way of bringing the rich to the same level as the have-nots. The basic problem . . ."

"Yes, an interesting point of view. Thank you, caller. We'll take a short break now for an update from the newsroom—"

Buckingham Palace was almost complete. It stood on a tray in the dining room. I dismantled some of the back walls, discovering that Grandmother Duncan had cheated by using Blu-Tack here and there. What I hadn't realized was the weight of the coins. A couple of handfuls dragged down the pockets of the bomber jacket. I transferred some to my jeans pockets and wondered if there'd be any other loose money—bills—around the house. The slightly crossed eyes of the two Burmese cats on the top of the bookshelf were watching me.

I made myself look through some of the dark rooms, afraid to put on any extra lights. This house had always seemed sinister to me; Pat's bloodthirsty jokes about Grandfather Duncan and missing dead bodies hadn't helped. "*She* makes him steal them," he'd say. "She hides them behind the sofa in the sitting room and gnaws on the bones while she's watching TV." "Oh yuk," I'd be going. Lil (trying not to laugh) would say something like, "Leave her alone, Pat. The poor woman, so anxious to be respectable, and so many skeletons in her closet." That expression really cracked Pat up.

I couldn't find any money. I took some more of Buckingham Palace, thinking how satisfying it would be to topple the rest to the floor. I didn't do it. Not because of Grandmother Duncan's months of work, but because I might want some more later.

City Folk

I headed for the city, toward Hindley Street. There'd be crowds to melt into. Cop cars were cruising King William Street. I kept my head down and walked swiftly. It really was true: my knee was going through a supple stage, there was no pain and I didn't limp. And no one took any notice of me when I joined the people drifting among the noise and lights of Hindley Street.

Except one. He was sprawled on a seat outside the café where half a lifetime ago I'd puked chocolate gelati and whipped cream. It was Shark Pelacci, someone from school I knew or rather took care not to know, not to make eye contact with, not to meet in an isolated spot when he and his gang were in roving-and-thumping mode.

Too late. There was eye contact. He shifted his head in a summoning movement. I found myself hesitating.

"Going anywhere," he said.

I shrugged. He kicked the leg of the chair next to him

so it moved away from the table. I sat down, as I was expected to, sprawling as he was, but every muscle tense and ready.

"On your own?" he asked after a while.

If I said yes, it might be a trap. If I said no, it might sound like an invitation for a brawl. "Yeah, right now," I settled for, in a noncommittal way.

"Me too," he said. "They're all outta town."

Fairly soon he asked me if I had any money. "A few dollars," I said. I didn't know how much I had.

"I'm waiting for Mel," he said, looking around, and suddenly she was there, before I had time to be ready. Melanie Gibbs, high priestess of the wild set at school, standing less than an arm's distance away, now sitting at the table crossing her legs slowly, short short skirt, looking me over in minute detail.

She took a cigarette from the pack on the table and lit it. "What's your name? Ian, isn't it? Ian something."

"Ian Ganty," I said. I had been able to keep my eyes on hers. I hadn't been terrorized into looking down and blushing and shuffling. But my forehead felt hot, and I brushed my hair back from it.

"Cool gloves," she said.

I'd forgotten them. My hands had been anchored in my pockets for ages, clenched around the twin weights of coins.

Shark said, "He's got some cash."

"Clever," she said admiringly, widening her eyes. They were surrounded by dark lines of kohl, and her skin was made up to a pearly paleness. Her hair was long and black and wild with pearl-colored tips. Jet-bead earrings hung to her shoulders. Still looking at her, I drew my other hand out of my pocket and flattened a handful of two-dollar coins on the table. There were twenty or thirty of them. A couple rolled off and jangled on the pavement. She laughed and bent to pick them up.

"Shee-yit," said Shark. "What'd you do, rob a church?"

"No. Buckingham Palace," I replied.

Now they were both laughing, hilariously, for several seconds, as if I'd made an amazing joke. Melanie was making patterns with the coins, still watching me. "So, why do you hang out with such dorks at school?" she asked. "Going to the library and stuff?"

"I'm trying to learn how to read."

They seemed to think even that one was quite good, but I was still wary. There was a strong chance I was being set up here.

"I'll have cheese and tomato. And salami," she said. "And a double cappuccino."

"Same here," said Shark. They were both looking at me.

"Sure," I said, finally clicking. I looked around, trying to remember if they came out to take orders. It didn't look like it. Another problem. It would be impossible to shovel all the coins back into my pocket when I got up, as if I expected them to steal the money when my back was turned, which I did expect, really. I compromised, gathering some of the coins to pay for the order, a little clumsily because of the gloves and because Melanie was watching my hands.

I glanced back outside while I was giving the order. They had their heads together, talking, and they didn't draw apart until I sat down again.

"Lotta cop noise out here," Shark said. He was right. The cops were cruising both in cars and on foot, very visible. I felt uneasy. For about half an hour I'd forgotten the cops.

"Move inside?" I suggested, and to my amazement they both stood up immediately, helped me gather up the rest of the coins and followed me—followed *me*—into the café.

"Why so many?" asked Melanie, meaning the police.

"Usual shit," Shark said. "Joy-riders. A holdup. Yeah, and some kids torched that rich guy's limo. Maybe they're looking for someone walking around with an empty gas can."

"Where'd you get those gloves?" Melanie's attention was back to me.

"Borrowed them," I said.

She held out her hand and I drew them off. They were too big for her. She shook her hands, looking regretful, and they slid off. I took them back.

The toasted sandwiches arrived, fragrant with the richness of cheese and tomato, and I realized I was starving. I got ready for the first huge bite, then stopped. The smell triggered a vivid memory. The scene unfolded: Jaz, the lasagna, the oven turned on hours ago, ST shut in the house, the house in flames. I stood up so fast my chair was flung over.

"Jeez. Are you sick?" Melanie said. "You're all white."

"I'm going." I raced out without looking back. I needed a taxi but it was pointless to flag one down in the crawling traffic of Hindley Street. I ran across the road and down a side street to North Terrace. Surely there'd be cabs hanging around the hotels there.

I found one almost immediately. "It's urgent," I shouted to the driver. We rocketed toward home with me gripping the edge of the seat, trying to banish the vision of ST trapped in a burning house, dreading what I might find.

Out

The house was as dark and solid as I'd left it. There were no screaming fire sirens and leaping flames. Only ST, really pleased to see me.

The oven was turned off. This was confusing. I wondered if I'd imagined Jaz arriving with the lasagna, and all the rest of that horrific sequence. No, I hadn't. The lasagna sat inside the oven, not cold, still tepid.

I ate some of it, standing beside the sink. Cold porridge would have tasted good to me by then. ST liked it, too. So, who turned the oven off? Had Lil been home? I walked through the house, turning on the lights as I went, apprehensive, not sure why.

Nothing else was changed. Lil's room was as I'd left it, with the lid of the little wooden box on her table standing open. It would have been closed for certain had Lil been here. I must have turned the oven off myself, automatically. Maybe when I was getting the kitchen matches to burn the remains of Gideon.

I saw myself in the long mirror, still wearing the jacket, the left-hand pocket weighted with coins, the other bulging with the gloves. My face was white, whiter than Melanie's, eyes drooping with tiredness. The image blurred. Gideon's face was there. "Getting rid of me is the hard part," he repeated.

I swayed. For a moment everything in the room went hazy. I moved toward Lil's bed. I wanted to curl up there and sleep. Tonight had gone on too long. And I hadn't managed to kill Gideon. He was still here.

"Get me a drink," Gideon said. "Something icy with a kick. With some teeth."

In the kitchen I made Lil's once-a-week, after-work-on-Friday mixture. Two shots of gin, one of dry vermouth, measured in a liquor glass. Three chunks of ice. A sliver of lemon skin made with the potato peeler. Stir for twelve seconds. Drink fast.

"Of course you didn't really kill me," Gideon said. "You *need* me. Since when have Shark and Melanie even noticed you before?"

I took the coins out of my pocket and piled them on the table by the sofa, then added to them the ones from my jeans pockets. They were evidence that I really had gone into my grandparents' house and dismantled the back wall of Buckingham Palace. That had really happened.

I needed this sort of proof about things. There was a haziness, an edge of unreality in my mind about the last three days.

The ride in Gideon's car? The only evidence for that was having no money left because of the taxi ride with ST. The bus holdup? It was clear I'd lost my gym gear and bag and library book somewhere, and somehow I'd gotten the scratch on my face that had been bad enough to bleed all over my pillowcase. Did that happen? If so, I couldn't remember what I'd done with the pillowcase, if I'd put it in the laundry basket, or left it on the floor in my room. The thought of that worried me, the perfection of the color balance marred by something so violently discordant.

I didn't go and check. I was aware of an unpleasant floating sensation. My head hit the cushions on the sofa.

"I can't believe this," said Gideon. "You've got this amazing out-of-it feeling, and you just want to sleep?"

It was a mixed sort of dream I had, sometimes with that frustrating wading-through-mud feeling when you can't make progress, other times with the feeling that everything's easy: you're flying. I'm running along the street. It's dark, and the houses are quiet. It's the same route I took earlier in the evening but this time ST's with me. "Go home!" I shout at her, making shooing movements with my hands, but she thinks it's a game and runs around me in circles, barking. A light appears in one of the dark houses so I run on, ST in the lead.

I'm at the Duncan house, looking at the shining white perfection of their garage doors. Buckingham Palace has crumpled and lies in golden fragments over the carpet. I have a can of paint and a brush. The paint is red and lustrous. But it's hard to form the words, because the brush is wide and I'm laughing so much, so I have to make the writing very large, across the whole width of the garage doors. BODY SNATCHER! Then I have to put the lid on the paint can, and wipe the brush and the dribbles of paint from the outside of the can with handfuls of grass, which are difficult to find because the Grandparents Duncan keep their lawn close-shaved. It's important the paint can isn't too messy, because I want to take it home with me, speeding back through the darkness.

Of course I didn't remember all this dream as soon as I woke up. It was bright in the living room, painfully bright with the sun beating through the windows.

Lil was there, bending over me, holding a steaming mug. She was frowning and smiling a little at the same time.

I felt ill as soon as I tried to sit up. I sank back and covered my eyes.

"I'm not surprised," Lil said. "I saw the gin bottle on the bench." I could hear her moving about, pulling curtains, darkening the room. A moment later she was tucking a blanket around me. "Sleep on," she said. "I'll ask all my questions later."

"I've got questions for you, too," I wanted to say, but it was easier to slide back into sleep.

Questions

Lil's note was propped on the coffee table. *I'm at the G. Duncans. They've had a break-in! I won't be long. WAIT HERE FOR ME. Love, L.*

"Wait here for me" looked like she meant it. It had overtones of a big reckoning to come. As for the Duncans' break-in, well, that was nothing to do with me. Grandmother Duncan couldn't have noticed the few steps and back walls I'd taken from Buckingham Palace. However, as I was searching the fridge for some food, I started to worry that I hadn't locked their front door when I left.

I made some fried lasagna on toast. There was nothing else to eat, not even an egg. I took the plate back to the sofa in the living room and turned on the television. I didn't want to have to think about anything.

Commercials on two channels. The third had the midday news so I left it on because there'd be a movie after. ST was beside me on the sofa, nosing toward the steaming lasagna, and I was so busy elbowing her away that I nearly missed it: center screen, *my gym bag*. It had been found, the news reporter said, at the scene of a crime. He mentioned the torching of a car.

Gym bags all look pretty much alike except to their owners, and I knew this was mine. The news reporter said that the police wanted to find the owner of the bag to help them with their inquiries.

I knew what they meant by the car burning. Shark and Melanie had mentioned it, and also I'd heard a radio talk show about it somewhere recently. That's all. And yet it was very vivid in my memory. Gas thrown from a bright silver can over the motor and the car's upholstery, into the trunk, over the wheels. Then people running, and a thrown flame, and *whoosh!*

I couldn't have been there. Suddenly I wasn't hungry, and gave ST the plate on the floor.

I was being pushed into the area I'd been trying to avoid: having to think. I wanted to avoid it because I was terrified by the fact that I couldn't distinguish what had really happened from imagined happenings—those things I'd written as Gideon adventures. The only thing I remembered clearly was destroying Gideon.

I remembered his mocking "Oh, really?" and shivered. I am not afraid, I told myself; I am shivering because I'm cold. My blue sweater was folded neatly on the arm of the sofa, by Lil, of course. As I pulled it on, I wondered what else she'd found when she arrived home this morning.

Her gloves and her leather jacket with the Grandparents Duncan keys in the pocket, for a start. The two-dollar coins.

Before I'd gone to sleep on the sofa, I'd emptied the coins from my jeans pockets and piled them on the table. The jacket I'd have probably tossed over a chair or onto the floor along with my sweater. There was no sign of either the coins or the jacket in the room.

Like a sleepwalker I wandered through the house. In Lil's wardrobe I found her jacket, exactly where it always was. The Grandparents Duncan keys were in the wooden box on her desk. My own house keys were hung in their usual place on one of the hooks inside the front door. I couldn't find the coins.

Maybe none of it had happened. I didn't really put on Lil's jacket and go to the Grandparents Duncan and take the coins and then meet Shark and Melanie on Hindley Street.

By now I was hurrying through the house, searching for some sort of answer. I was getting colder and colder, and my sneakers had disappeared. I went back into the living room and turned on the heater, hunching over it like an old sick man. It was then I heard a key in the front door, and Lil walked in.

"Hello, darling," she said. "It's freezing, isn't it? Why not put the kettle on for some tea?" I stared at her, searching for something in her face, some sign of the metamorphosis I'd seen in her outside the casino. There was nothing. She was the same. The same saggy sweater but now with some splotches of white paint. The same calm face, no earrings, no eye shadow. One eyebrow lifting as she realized I was staring.

"I'm not going to shout at you," she said, "but I do need to know what's been happening. How you got that dreadful scratch on your face would do for a start."

I went into the kitchen and made tea, very slowly. I could hear Lil in the living room talking to ST. The early afternoon sky was darkening and a cold misty rain was thrown against the windows by the wind.

"A gathering storm," I heard Lil say. I poured two mugs of tea and took them into the living room.

"The Duncans arrived home from Clare this morning,"

Lil said. She was sitting on the armchair by the heater, her elbows on her knees, her hands clasped around her mug of tea. "Someone had been into the house and smashed Grandmother Duncan's Buckingham Palace to bits. Two-dollar coins were everywhere. And they'd left graffiti on the garage doors. Bright red paint."

"What sort of graffiti?" I asked. My lips felt stiff.

"Nothing very decorative. Not the normal signing stuff. This was malicious. When I arrived, Grandfather Duncan was trying to stick newspaper over it."

"Did they call the police?"

"No."

There was a long silence. I knew I had to say something. "Why didn't they call the police? What did the graffiti say?"

She didn't hesitate. "I think you know already, Ian."

"Why would I know?" I shouted. "I didn't have anything to do with it."

She went on as if I'd said nothing. "It was unkind of you, Ian. Grandfather Duncan was never personally involved in that missing body business, and it was a very long time ago."

I was leaning forward, holding my bare toes in my hands. Cold as my fingers were, they were still warmer than my feet. I could feel an anger in my chest building so it was hard to breathe.

"Ian, why don't you find some socks? Where are your shoes?"

How could she be putting on this act of being so calm and gentle? I stood up.

I wasn't me. Gideon was giving me my words and my anger. "Listen to me for once. Stop all this being nice shit. I wasn't anywhere near their place. I don't know what you're talking about. You've finally gone loopy and started living one of your stupid TV scripts. Just leave me alone."

I strode from the room and through the kitchen and out the back door. I was still not breathing properly. I stood with the rain hitting my face. Gideon had shown me that Lil had been trying to trick me. She had been trying to make me believe that something I *knew* had only been a dream had really happened.

The cardboard box of plants from Grandmother Duncan was disintegrating in the rain. I gave it a kick and noticed that ST had continued to use it as an outhouse. There was something else in the box, something pressed down between the earth and the cardboard side.

I fished it out. It was a bundle made up of Lil's leather gloves, glued grotesquely out of shape by paint. Red paint. I could smell it.

Jacqueline

I went from the back door directly to my bedroom so I wouldn't have to face Lil again. All my anger and fury had dissolved instantly when I'd found the gloves. What I felt now was total terror. It was clear I didn't have any control over my life

"Well, Ian, what was so bad about last night? You had a good time, didn't you? You enjoyed Shark and Melanie hanging on your words and you loved being able to chuck money around.

"Admit it. You missed me after you killed me. You brought me back to life because secretly *you really want to be me.*"

I'd set out innocently to complete a school holiday task, and I'd ended up with this monster. I didn't believe I was being haunted by a ghost. I didn't believe I was being taken over by some ancestor. I didn't believe I was re-living some former incarnation of myself.

So, either Gideon was some deep down hidden part of

me finally boiling to the surface, or I'd gone overboard with my own invention. There was only one way to test this. If I'd invented one, I could invent another.

I needed to create someone strong enough to replace Gideon, someone who interested me so much that Gideon's power would shrivel to nothing.

Who would it be? I started to flick through Lil's baby-naming book, and found "Jacqueline: from Old French; *the supplanter.*" Perfect.

Jacqueline, I decided, was a boarder at a girls' school. This was because I didn't have time to think up a family for her. Not right now, anyway. Maybe later.

I started my notes. *Jacqueline. White-blonde hair, green eyes, heart-shaped face, small sharp chin. Wears purple, a long flowing coat with a tasseled hood. Her hair swings forward and covers her face at each side when she peers into her crystal ball.*

What? Crystal ball? I hit the delete button and got rid of the last seven words. It was the purple coat that had done it. I should dress her in jeans like everyone else. She could have a long purple scarf with jet beads threaded into the fringe at each end. But I'd already decided that Jacqueline's strength would spring partly from a mystical source. She would have premonitions, visions of the future, something like that.

At school: member of the rowing team. Long arms and legs, very good at rowing.

I was starting to be able to picture her, but she needed a setting. I thought about the school. Its grounds were like the ones at our school: an area of lawn surrounded by shady trees with benches under them; a sheltered quadrangle with fixed tables and chairs; a covered walkway from the library to the main school. It was spring, a warm day, and the school was unusually quiet. It was exam time. Girls sat in the quadrangle or under the trees looking through notes or giving each other last-minute tests in subdued voices. I could see Jacqueline. She was walking slowly through the covered walkway from the library, her head bent, holding a large book against her chest with both arms. She crossed the quadrangle, and headed toward the boarding house, an elegant old two-story building with curving steps up to a wide veranda.

Jacqueline was worried. There was the history exam in the afternoon, and that was worrying enough. But she was aware of something else, a niggling kind of dread that was shadowing everything. Something unpleasant was going to happen.

She tried to shrug off the shadow, tried to concentrate on the dozens of past lives she'd studied during the year of history lessons. The confining medieval world, she said to herself. The confusion of church and state in people's minds. The desire to find new worlds. The disaster of imperialism. The horrors of life as a settler in alien territories. All those countless millions of people, every one of them aware and unique, all linked in the giant design of history—

Hang on, I told myself, you're getting carried away here. Then I realized what was happening. Suddenly it was clear to me that Jacqueline's power would come from her awareness of all her past lives. The reincarnation idea. She was becoming interesting. My experiment was starting to work.

I saw her enter the boarding house, and pause at the grid of pigeonholes for the boarders' mail. There were no letters for her, but there was a package for Marion, her roommate. It was unusual for Marion to get mail because she went home on weekends. Marion never bothered to check the pigeonholes. Jacqueline decided to take the package up to the room they shared.

It was a small post office mailing package, no stamp or postmark, and Jacqueline could see where it had been neatly slit open then stapled shut by someone in the school office. Jacqueline stopped halfway up the stairs and clung to the banisters for a moment. The dread, the shadow, was no longer just an itch. It was very strong. It centered on the package. She could see the person writing the address on it, see him sticking down the flap. She'd never seen him in her life before, but at that moment she knew who he was, and what was in the package.

And then other things about Marion, how she'd been behaving over the last few weeks, suddenly made sense. Jacqueline felt sick with anxiety about what to do next. She knew Marion wouldn't be in their room yet, wouldn't have finished her morning math exam. A decision could wait for an hour.

But Marion was in their room. She was lying on her bed. Instinctively Jacqueline held the package behind her back, and stayed leaning against the door she'd closed after her.

Marion rolled onto her back and shielded her eyes with her forearm.

"What about your exam?" Jacqueline asked. "Are you sick?"

It took ages for Marion to answer. "Couldn't be stuffed," she said.

"You're crazy."

Marion propped herself on one elbow, squinting at Jacqueline. "You're becoming a pain," she said at last. "And why're you just standing there? What are you hiding behind your back?"

"Just a library book," Jacqueline said, but at that moment she felt her grip on the package loosen, and it slid to the floor.

Marion was off the bed and tearing open the package. "A present," she said, a gloat in her voice. It was an oblong plastic case containing a fountain pen, a note folded around it. Marion read the note and dropped it on the floor. It was the pen that interested her.

Jacqueline didn't need to pick up the note to know what it said. *Good luck with your exams from Gideon.* She also knew that the pen wouldn't write, because the space for the ink cartridge was stuffed with amphetamines, tiny tablets of speed.

And she knew that at around six o'clock, when Marion's parents arrived home from work, they'd find their video recorder missing and some other household toys, probably Marion's mother's jewelry too.

The speed was payment for keys and instructions for disabling the burglar alarm. Jacqueline knew all this as if she had a video camera on Marion's thought processes.

So this was the unpleasant event: her involvement with this destructive stuff. Jacqueline cursed her mysterious powers. Having the knowledge meant she had to act.

In the meantime, however, she decided to say nothing. Sooner or later she'd have her chance, and Gideon would be history.

Library Book

That was not meant to happen.

Gideon definitely wasn't supposed to be crashing in on Jacqueline's story. I couldn't believe it. I left the word processor and walked around the room.

It was as if Gideon was showing his power over me. This was going to lead to a confrontation between Jacqueline and Gideon, and I hadn't planned on that happening, either.

I was afraid that Jacqueline wasn't going to be strong enough. Her last few sentences sounded brave, but when I went back to the screen and read them again, I thought they had a hint of desperation. She knew his power as well as I did. Of course she did. I made her up.

"Ian!" It was Lil's voice, startling, unreal, calling me from the hallway outside. "There's someone here to see you."

Instantly I was on guard. The watchers from the car outside had finally decided to make their move.

Face them down. Don't admit anything, I told myself. Or rather, Gideon told me. I was aware of his presence. I didn't even try to fight it.

The visitor was not who I expected. In the living room stood the Skull. He was wearing a long droopy raincoat and strange woven sandals. In his hands he held the English cloth cap he always wore outside. His bald head gleamed with its usual weird greenish light that I'd always thought was the reflection from the computer screen in the library. His eyes were even deeper in their shadows.

"Mr. Skillington said something about a missing library book, Ian," Lil said.

"Yes?" I replied.

There was a silence. They were both looking at me as if I was supposed to say more.

The Skull spoke. "The police contacted me again. I was concerned." He cleared his throat, and glanced at Lil.

"It's just a book," I said. "Anyway, I'm not that interested in reading anymore."

"Ian!" Lil said in a bossy don't-speak-to-your-elders-and-betters-like-that tone of voice that really got up my nose.

"Well, why should he care if a book is missing? They're not *his* books anyway. They belong to the school. He always goes on as if he owns them personally."

I left the room at that point and went into the kitchen and opened the fridge.

"I'm sorry he spoke to you like that," Lil said. "I don't know what to say. He's not himself."

They obviously moved into the hallway and were standing by the front door, because their voices were muffled. I couldn't hear the words. They spoke together for several minutes.

So, Lil thought I was not myself. Maybe she didn't realize she had a new Ian to get to know.

She'd been shopping. The fridge was full of packages wrapped in the white paper the Greek deli at the market always used, and the fruit bowl on the table held oranges and small fat bananas.

I heard the front door close as the Skull left. Then Lil was in the kitchen. "What's going on?" she demanded.

"Nothing." I wondered what the Skull had said to her. I didn't care. I wasn't afraid of her.

"Mr. Skillington said the cops phoned him twice about this library book. The first time he told them he'd check the records. But he said to me that he had no trouble remembering who'd borrowed it last. He said students like you stand out from the rest. Students who are keen and intelligent readers, he said."

"What a privilege. Fancy being memorable to someone like the Skull."

She ignored this. "He's worried, and I am too, about why the cops would go to so much trouble over a lost school library book. It was the Criminal Investigation Department that phoned the second time, not just someone from lost property. He felt he had to tell them your name."

"The Skull's getting carried away. His life's so boring he has to invent a drama."

Her voice was cold and angry. "I want to know what's been happening, Ian. For a start, why did you stay here when you were supposed to be at Zelda's?"

"I don't need a babysitter."

Something about my tone seemed to put her on guard. She stepped back so she had the sink top to lean on. It was as if she needed to rally her strength. I was winning.

"Ian, what's going on? I don't know you at all. First you mess up the Duncans', and now this . . . it's like you're living some secret life."

"A secret life? Well, what about your secret life? I saw

you, on Tuesday night, outside the casino. You probably thought I'd never find out. But I saw you."

I watched her carefully. She was very, very good. I could learn from her. Her face showed total incomprehension and amazement. Her voice matched. "What do you mean, you saw me outside the casino? I was staying at Josie's in Victor Harbor. Nowhere near the city. You know that."

"I saw you, on Tuesday night, dressed up like a model, outside the casino, with some guy."

"Me, dressed like a model? You imagined it." Her denial was so convincing it would have succeeded with anyone else.

"Look, I don't care. Your life is your business. I don't want to interfere. Just make sure you return the favor. Don't interfere with mine."

At that moment ST crashed through the cat-flap in the back door. She greeted me as if I'd been away for months, leaping up, trying to land a lick on my chin. "Get off me!" I shouted. "I can't stand fawning dogs!" I kicked her.

She squealed and backed off. Her ears were flattened into their alarm position, sticking straight out on each side of her head.

"You *brute*," Lil hissed. She shoved me aside and knelt to comfort ST.

Suddenly I was Ian again, horrified at what was happening.

"Just get out of my sight," said Lil.

I couldn't reply. There was nothing I could say. I retreated to my room and locked the door.

I knew that Jacqueline had to be strong enough. She just had to be.

On the Beach

Jacqueline knew there was growing hostility between her and Marion, but she also knew that she must go on pretending they were best friends. It was the only way she could get to Gideon.

Now Marion was trying to discourage her from coming home with her for the weekend. "Mom's too distressed by the burglary to have anyone extra staying," she said.

Jacqueline didn't believe her. She went downstairs and telephoned Marion's mother. "It's really kind of you to ask me to stay when you're upset by the burglary and all. Are you sure it's okay if I come?"

"Jacqueline, my dear, we're looking forward to seeing you. Don't worry. I'm not at all upset." She told Jacqueline that the joke was on the thieves, because they'd stolen the cheap brass and glass copies of her real jewelry, which was in the safe at work. "Can you imagine their faces when they find out? I said to James, that really makes it all worthwhile! So, see you Friday night.

I'm glad the burglary won't stop you from visiting."

Jacqueline went upstairs and found Marion, who had played sick all day and missed both her biology and French exams. "There's a message from your mother. She's fine. Everything's sorted out about the robbery and she's expecting us both for the weekend."

Marion looked angry. Jacqueline couldn't resist adding, "It sounds like the cops found the thieves and got everything back."

That made Marion sit up and stare at Jacqueline, until the light became too strong for her eyes and she had to shield them with her hands.

"If you're sick, why didn't they put you in sick bay?"

Marion shrugged. She lay back on the bed. "I just pretended I had the runs all night. Too weak and dizzy to get up today. So don't worry. You won't catch anything deadly. Worse luck." Her voice was bitter.

Jacqueline shivered. It was going to be a long and difficult weekend.

On Friday night, Marion's mother and father picked them up at six. By then they'd learned that Marion had missed all her exams and they were worrying whether she'd get enough credits from previous months' work. "She must rest," they said to each other, and let the girls pick up six videos on the way home.

By seven the parents had gone out, and Jacqueline and Marion were alone. Marion was restless. Every ten minutes she made a phone call, got no answer and hung up looking discontented. After a couple of hours she stopped phoning. She lay along the sofa and fell asleep. She had not spoken a word to Jacqueline all day.

Jacqueline didn't mind. This was exactly as she'd expected. Tomorrow would be the tricky day.

Saturday, by midday, Marion was carefully dressed in black jeans and a jacket and long earrings. She had black eye pencil drawn around her eyes. Jacqueline wore dark blue jeans and the fleecy sweater in strong green that matched her eyes, and her purple scarf with the jet beads knotted into the fringes. She stood behind Marion as they said good-bye to her mother. It was obvious that Marion wanted to shake Jacqueline off, but how could she with her mother waving them good-bye, so pleased to see Marion going out for the afternoon with her friend?

"I wish you'd get lost," said Marion as soon as they were on the sidewalk. Jacqueline pretended not to hear. Marion was walking quickly, bent forward. They reached the beach in record time.

It was cold, a south wind bending the sand grasses and flinging grains of sand into their eyes. Marion hunched her shoulders, looking left and right, and when she saw that the beach was empty apart from a couple with an Irish setter far away at the other end, she headed for the shelter of the sand dunes. Jacqueline sat down beside her. Marion was flexing her fingers, still looking from side to side. "He won't meet me if he sees you here," she said.

Jacqueline believed he'd arrive twice as fast, because he'd think she was a new customer. It was just a matter of waiting.

"Why do you have to hang around like this?" Marion tried again. "Haven't you heard that three's a crowd? Are you jealous that I've got a boyfriend and you don't?"

"A *boyfriend*? Is that what you call him? He's just using you. Got you hooked and made you tell him how to rob your parents' house."

Marion looked agitated. "You can't prove that . . ." she started.

"And I bet he's trying to get you to deal at school. What

a great boyfriend. Yeah, I'm desperate with jealousy."

Marion was almost in tears. She couldn't stop shaking. "You don't know *anything*," she said.

There was a voice above them, from higher on the dune. "I want to talk to you, Marion."

Marion jumped to her feet.

"You owe me," the voice continued. "That jewelry was rubbish. Not worth five cents."

"But you got the VCR and things." It was as if she'd forgotten Jacqueline, or now didn't care what she heard.

"A hundred bucks is all that's worth these days. You said there was good jewels and stuff."

"Well, there was! There was!" Obviously Marion's mother hadn't told her about the cheap copies. "Look, Gideon, maybe you were ripped off."

"Ripped off?" Jacqueline could see his shadow advancing across the sand and knew he was at the edge of the embankment. "Nobody rips me off. Like you're not going to rip me off. I want those pills back. All of them. You didn't earn them. Your information was way less than textbook."

Jacqueline stood so she was next to Marion, who was quivering and terrified. Gideon kept his fierce gaze on Marion, and Jacqueline had the stunning sensation of being invisible. She linked her arm through Marion's to give her strength. "You're pathetic," she said upward to Gideon.

Gideon said, "Who's this silly bitch?" at the same time as Jacqueline felt and could hardly believe Marion's struggling to get free from her linking arm. Jacqueline released her hold immediately. She realized she was going to have to win this one on her own.

"Ignore her, Gideon," Marion was saying. "She's just someone from school. She thinks she's some kind of witch."

"A witch," said Gideon with mock admiration. "Let's burn her, then." He held out his arm, and his hand flared as sunlight caught the shining steel knife. He bent his knees and sprang at Jacqueline.

At the point of his landing, he was as vulnerable as a gymnast landing after a bench vault. And Jacqueline was ready, shoulders pushed forward. She knocked him over as he teetered for balance. The knife spun from his hand into hers.

She held the knife. Long arms, long legs, she locked him to the ground and laughed in his face. "See what I mean? Pathetic. Sad little bully."

He was pinned down as by a praying mantis. She swung her jet beads and he swore as they stung his eyes. But he was a wasp, strong and vicious and wiry. And something else. He gave off a heat like the fabled furnace of hell. Jacqueline shook but she wouldn't give in, wouldn't drop the knife.

She heard Marion scream but didn't care whose side she was on. The scream came from so far off, it didn't matter anymore.

Gideon was transformed from wasp to amber-eyed trickery. Jacqueline was armed with centuries of loathing. They were spinning in open space, somewhere plain and uncomplicated where these battles have always been fought. Exhausted, Jacqueline saw her chance. As she lunged toward him with the knife and saw the redness flash around them, she wondered if it was worth it. How many more times? And to defend such worthless victims?

Part Three

Visitors

I saw this fight between Jacqueline and Gideon as the legendary battle between good and evil. It wasn't hard to work out where I got that idea.

When Jaz was thirteen she went through a religious phase. She used to collect me on Sunday mornings and make me go to church with her. It was when I was having knee operations and quite often I'd be on crutches or even in a wheelchair.

I complained about going. I repeated Lil's comment, that she thought good old kindness to others was much better than the rules of organized religion. But I didn't refuse to go. I'd secretly caught some of Jaz's enthusiasm for the ceremony and the mystery.

Then Jaz joined the church choir. She had a pure soprano voice. All the religious songs moved her very much. "Oh kingly head surrounded, with mocking cro – own of thorns," she would sing, in the street, her eyes misting. I wished she wouldn't sing out loud like that. We made a strange-looking pair as it was.

I diverted her into conversation. "How do you know God exists anyway?"

"He just does."

"But how can you prove it?"

Jaz was scornful. "I don't have to *prove* it." She said only boring people went around trying to prove and disprove things, that things were much more interesting when they were mysterious. Then she was off again. "Oh kingly head . . ."

I was worried that she'd decide to become a nun and disappear behind convent walls forever. Maybe that was why I kept on going to church with her: so I could check on her enthusiasm to make sure it wasn't getting too extreme. I realized some time later that her fervor had more to do with a crush on the choir mistress. But I, too, liked the words of the songs, the phrases in the sermons, and the prayers. "Liberate me O Lord from eternal death and thy dreadful wrath," I found myself murmuring as I whizzed down the aisle in my wheelchair.

But the dreadful wrath arrived anyway. My parents were killed. Their memorial service was the last time I ever went into a church. I don't remember if I sang any hymns or took part in the prayers that day. I felt brain dead. I found myself believing something that Jaz had told me, that there was such a thing as a force of pure evil. It seemed to me that evil really did exist, and that it could reach out and strike at random.

Lil said it wasn't true that there was such a thing as pure evil. It couldn't exist without people. People behaved evilly, or they behaved well. Most people wavered and did a bit of both.

My mind was fixed on Jaz's idea of pure evil and pure good as I splashed the bright red paint around my room when Jacqueline won her battle over Gideon. They weren't *people* anymore. Gideon symbolized evil in my story and Jacqueline symbolized good, just as my red paint symbolized the death of Gideon.

Then it was over. I was exhausted. I must have slept for ages, because the next thing I knew Lil was banging on the door, asking if I was all right and telling me it was nearly lunchtime. A whole night had gone, and most of the morning.

I unlocked the door, not sure what sort of mood she'd be in after yesterday. She looked around the room. "I don't know if it's an improvement or not," she said.

I'd fallen asleep on the floor in the pool of paint left when the can tipped over. The walls were covered in arcs of ruby drops from the swishing paintbrush. "I had to kill him," I said to Lil. "He was taking over."

She shook her head, frowning slightly. "You'll have to explain. But later." She helped me take off my paint-glued sweater. I felt weak. "Hop in the shower," she said. "I'll make lunch and we'll talk then."

It was bliss—the soothing hiss of the shower on my skin, and Lil there, just in the other room, not really angry now. Me being me.

Lil was making sandwiches, ham and tomato and cheese and lettuce. "Real basic," she said.

I was taking the first bite when I noticed, outside the front windows, the dark blue car with the shaded windows. There it was again. They weren't giving up. I'd dealt with Gideon, but there was still all the police stuff to go.

Then there was a bang on the front door. I realized something was missing: no eager barking. "Where's ST?" I asked, putting the sandwich down.

"She hasn't come back home."

I remembered Gideon's savage kick. "I'll go out and look for her," I said.

The door knocker sounded again. I followed Lil to the door. Outside stood Melanie and Shark. They seemed doubtful when they saw Lil, and even more doubtful when they saw me. They looked like creatures that shouldn't ever be out in the daylight. But I was feeling far too self-conscious to take in any details. I don't have the sort of hair that looks good when it's rubbed dry with a towel, and I was wearing a ratty old sweatsuit. Even if I'd put on Pat's red dressing gown I could have felt I had some style. The only thing I noticed about Melanie, apart from the growing distaste in her eyes, was that she was wearing black leather gloves with the cuffs rolled back over her wrists.

"Won't you come inside?" Lil said.

"We just wanted to see . . . ah Ian . . . ah about Buckingham Palace," Shark started, but Melanie was pulling his arm and making him leave. I couldn't find any words to say. I watched them go. They'd know now they'd been right about me all along.

Lil was back at the dining table. "You haven't touched your sandwiches yet," she said.

"Well, thanks very much," I shouted. "You got them to run right off, didn't you?"

"I invited them in," Lil said.

"When my friends come around, they don't want to be invited in to some family tea party sit-around-the-table thing."

"Ian. If you're desperate to go through some goddamn angry stage, go for it. Just leave me out of it, okay?"

She stood up and walked out. I heard her go into her room and slam the door.

I sat down at the table, and looked at the platter of sandwiches, and thumped my fist down as hard as I could in the middle of them.

I hadn't won. Gideon was still there. He'd alienated Jaz, and Lil, and ST, and now he was having another go at Lil. It was only paint on the walls of my room, not blood. In this sort of war, symbols didn't count.

Detectives

Two policemen arrived. The older one introduced himself as Detective Inspector Tring. The other cop, Detective Samuels, was a version of the Skull: totally bald, but much younger. He was carrying my gym bag. They asked to see Lil. Not her by name, but my "guardian."

Now that it had happened, they'd actually arrived, I felt quite calm. I even recognized a tinge of defiance which could grow much stronger if I let it. Gideon was lurking.

Lil looked pale and tired as she invited them in. She led them toward the table. They saw the squashed sandwiches. Without a word Lil picked up the platter and took it into the kitchen, and I heard it land on the bench with a crash.

Samuels put my gym bag on the table. "Is this yours?" I nodded. "Where did you see it last?"

I hesitated. Telling the truth would put me into that quagmire of questions. Why hadn't I reported the bus holdup? Where was my guardian that night? You mean she went on vacation and just left you alone?

I glanced at Lil's face but her eyes wouldn't meet mine and she looked fierce. She was probably on the point of putting me in foster care anyway.

"It was stolen from me on a bus."

"Why didn't you report it?"

I shrugged. Samuels and Tring exchanged glances. "What bus?" Tring asked.

I looked at Lil's hard face again, and swallowed. Here we go. "The Magill Road bus. It was about half past six on Tuesday night."

"What happened?" prompted Samuels. When I looked at him more closely, I realized he shaved his head.

"A guy hiding at the back of the bus asked the driver to hand over the money. He said he had a gun." Lil was looking at me now, eyes wide. "We were at this terminal thing at the top of Magill Road. I was on the bus by mistake. I was waiting to get back to town."

"You got on the *wrong bus*?" Lil asked.

Don't land me in it, I begged her silently. "Yes," I said out loud. I told the detectives about being forced to hand my gym bag to the gunman, about falling, and finding the bus gone a few minutes later.

"This happened on Tuesday night," said Tring. "It's now Friday. Why didn't you report it right away?"

This, of course, was the question.

"It was because of the bus driver," I said. "I could tell he thought I was part of it. Like helping the guy with the gun. I was afraid."

"Well, you were right about that," Samuels said. "Now, tell me what the guy with the gun said."

They made me go over it again and again, who said what and when, exact descriptions of the gunman.

"I still don't know why you were on that bus," said

Tring. "Bright kids like you don't just get on the wrong bus. Wrong side of the road, too, if you were heading home."

This was Lil's fault. She'd put the doubt in their minds. "I was following *her*. She told me she was somewhere else but I saw her, all dressed up, outside the casino, getting into a car. So I followed her."

"You followed her in a *bus*?" Tring was laughing. "You're not planning on a career in the force, I hope?"

Lil's voice was icy. "Ian thinks he saw me outside the casino. He's already asked me about this. So I think you can believe him."

I couldn't work out from this if she was admitting she was outside the casino or still trying to cover it up. I didn't have time to think. Samuels asked me what happened after the bus holdup. "I came back here."

"How?"

"Walked."

Again they exchanged glances. It sounded unlikely even to me. It was hard to believe I'd walked that far.

"You didn't go to a car park in Mile End and help rob a motorist and then set fire to his car?"

"No!"

"Well, that's where we found your bag. And the motorist, the one with the burnt car, he describes you. Exactly." Samuels stood up suddenly and thrust the gym bag into my face. "Go on, kid, smell it. Smell the gasoline. That bring back any memories?"

Lil was standing, hostile. "That's intimidation!"

The sudden strong gas fumes were making me choke. Samuels put the bag on the table and sat down. "Arsehole pigs," I said.

"Ian," Lil said quietly, sitting down herself.

"I had nothing to do with that car burning," I shouted, but of course it was hard for me to sound convincing.

And it was now far too late. Stupid. Should have been denying everything all along.

Detective Samuels's mobile phone beeped. He turned his back to us and spoke to it quietly. Detective Inspector Tring looked at Lil. "We'll be off now," he said. "Could I have a word with you before we go, Ms. Ganty?"

Lil and the two detectives talked together on the veranda. I went into Lil's room, a good place for eavesdropping.

I was just in time to see Jaz coming in the gate with ST in her arms. "Hello, Aunt Lil," she said. "I've brought ST back. I won't stay, since you've got visitors." She held out ST to Lil, who took a step backward. I could see a wide stretch bandage around ST's middle.

"Thanks, Jaz, but don't go just yet. Wait inside. I want a word with you."

I dodged back into the living room, knowing I'd have to face Jaz. I couldn't stay hidden in Lil's room or Lil would know I'd been trying to listen.

Jaz put ST on the living room floor. She flicked a piece of paper onto the table. "That's the vet's receipt," she said. "I paid."

I fetched one of the mangled sandwiches from the kitchen and held it out to ST.

"She's not hungry," Jaz said stonily. "I already tried to feed her."

After a long time, ST glanced up at me. Her ears were drooped down as far as they would go. She took a couple of steps toward me, her legs bent so much that her chest brushed the carpet, then two more.

"It's all right, ST," I said. "It's me. It's Ian. I promise."

Another step, and then I could pick her up. She yelped with the pressure of my hands near her bandage but then she was nestling against my chest and trying for a tongue kiss. "Hello, dogbreath," I said. "I'm really sorry."

Jaz was sitting straight, looking at me coldly. "You did that to her, didn't you," she said. "You total little shit."

And then Lil was back. The cops were gone. "Now look," she said to Jaz. "You obviously colluded with Ian to lie to your mother and fix it so he could stay here on his own. What was going on?"

"I'm sorry, Aunt Lil." Jaz was still looking at me with that hating face. "You'll have to ask him."

"You can't blame it all on Ian. You were supposed to arrange with Zelda—"

"I know I was supposed to! And I've said I'm sorry." She looked at Lil, then headed for the door. "I wasn't to know he'd choose just this week to turn into some kind of *monster*."

I shivered, and clung to ST.

Telling

So. It was now just Lil and me, staring at each other across the living room.

"What did they say to you, out on the veranda?"

It took her a moment or two to start speaking, as if she had to sort her words. "They said they were leaving you here in my care, for the present. I might have to take you in to be fingerprinted." Her voice was abrupt. She stood up and headed for her room. "I'm going to phone Jen. Don't go out." Her door closed.

Jen was her best friend. I couldn't believe that she could go off and have a chat with one of her pals while all this was going on. Then I remembered. Jen was a lawyer.

It was raining again. ST was in her basket by the heater. I ate some of the squashed sandwiches and then threw the rest away. I wandered into my room and looked at the walls. The red paint glistened mockingly. Ha, ha—fooled you. I considered painting the whole room black. I wondered if Lil or Jaz would ever speak normally to me again.

Lil seemed calmer after the phone call, but her face was still grim. "There's something I want to clear up first of all. This supposed sighting of me at the casino—when was it? Around six, Tuesday night? Well, at six thirty Josie and I were arriving at the Whaler's Inn for a dinner meeting. You tell me how I could get from Adelaide to Victor Harbor in under half an hour. And forty or more high school teachers can back up my alibi. It wasn't me, Ian. You made a mistake. I don't have some glamorous secret life. With me, what you see is what you get. No secrets. Okay?"

I didn't answer. She sounded convincing. I tried to picture the woman I'd seen but in my mind she'd become unalterably Lil. It was another question mark to add to all my others.

"So what happened between you and Jaz? Did you have a fight? Is that why you wouldn't go to stay with her and Zelda?"

I shrugged. I couldn't tell her why Jaz hated me.

She sighed. "Okay. Well, what about all this stuff the police are trying to pin on you? Is there any chance we can have a talk about that?" Lil was getting impatient, I could tell. I was feeling as if my jaw was wired shut.

She waited for a moment, then went on. "It's the description from the man whose car was burned that's the problem for the cops. He described you so exactly, the same description that the bus driver gave. Look, Ian, if you'd just tell me what happened, we can sort something out. You won't talk to me. I feel as if I'm swimming in jelly."

My voice worked at last. "I don't know what happened! Stop crowding me!" I was shouting.

She looked at me wearily, as if that stranger was back. "Oh please, Ian, not now."

I took some deep breaths, and concentrated. "It's all right," I said after a moment. "I'm not . . ."

"You're not what?"

"It's nothing. I'm sorry." But it wasn't nothing. It was a really big breakthrough for me. For the first time I had a glimmer of the possibility that I might be able to control Gideon.

She let it go. "So, the police can see that possibly you were an innocent victim in the bus holdup, but they're convinced you were part of the car burning, somehow. And there's something else they're suspicious about."

"What?" I felt panicky. Surely they couldn't know about Grandmother Duncan's Buckingham Palace?

"They think you had something to do with a car that was stolen from around the corner. Apparently it was taken on a joyride down Port Road, chased by a patrol car, and then abandoned."

She said this last sentence in a dead calm voice. It had the same effect on me, a dead calm dread that I'd never escape this nightmare. I flopped back onto the sofa with my eyes closed and listened to Lil's voice continuing.

"It was when Jaz arrived on the veranda with ST. Samuels stopped Jaz as she was coming inside and patted ST. He said he liked silky terriers. Then, right in front of me, he fished a plastic bag out of his pocket and dropped into it a couple of hairs he'd tweaked out of ST. I couldn't believe it. Then he asked me if you could drive. It seems they found silky terrier fur in the abandoned car. They're going to see if it matches up with ST's." Lil was still talking in this calm voice, not even looking at me. Now she came over to the sofa, sat beside me and took hold of my hand. "Please tell me they just made a wild guess and got it wrong. You wouldn't go riding in a stolen car, Ian? With or without ST?"

They were talking about the night of Gideon's car. Of course, ST had been in the car. The fur samples would match. They'd only have to fingerprint me to know that I'd been there for sure, too.

I didn't know what to say to Lil. But I think she could read my face. "Who's been involving you in their craziness, Ian?"

I shook my head.

"Was it those two who visited you this morning?"

Shark and Melanie. "No," I said. "They don't have anything to do with anything. They're just kids from school. They only came around to get money, anyway." I had to accept that. I was deceiving myself if I thought they were interested in me, even if I had been in Gideon-persona that night. The only gleam of comfort was in the fact that Melanie had copied my gloves.

"I heard," Lil said in a dry voice. "They wanted some more from Buckingham Palace."

It was clear she'd figured out I'd been spreading around some of the two-dollar coins from Grandmother Duncan's. But she didn't pursue this now. "The thing is, Ian, I convinced those cops to leave you with me, that you and I had a good relationship and that you would be able to talk to me."

There was a long silence. I could see it stretching out and putting a huge space between us. I knew this was a critical moment. If I couldn't get Lil to understand, nobody else would.

The wind howled. I watched the faded petals from the flowering cherry next door swirl through the air like a blizzard and cling to the wet path in snowdrifts.

"Would it help," Lil said, "if you wrote it down? You're good at writing things."

"Who said?"

"The Skull told me. I knew anyway."

I left the Skull information to think about later. I remembered all the pages of Gideon's story that I'd burned, and wondered if they would have made any sense to Lil. Well, it was too late. I would have to start all over again.

"It was a school project," I said. "Inventing a character. I invented Gideon. He was dark-haired and always wore black and never anything with labels on. He walked like a cat and didn't give a stuff about anyone . . ."

Lil Loses It

They were still watching me. I could see the dark plainclothes car in its usual place across the road, out of the direct glow of the streetlight but still in a good position to see everyone who left our house. They didn't trust Lil to keep me home, it seemed.

It was dark now. Nearly two hours had gone by as I told Lil the story of Gideon and me. She listened with total attention. I started to feel the pleasure of controlling the story. As Gideon became a believable character for Lil, he lost, at the same time, his power over me.

I told her how he'd twice sprung back to life after I'd thought I'd killed him, and how each time his control of me had been more subtle, more difficult for me to recognize or predict. And I ended the story by telling her about his last intrusion earlier this afternoon—the first time I'd been able to stop him taking over.

I don't know if she understood, or even believed me. After I'd finished talking, she said nothing for a while.

The room darkened. Then she went into the kitchen, saying, "Pull down the blinds, will you, Ian?" That was when I saw the car parked in the street.

I wandered into the kitchen, hoping to work out from Lil's face what she was thinking. She was grilling lamb chops and making a salad, no readable expression on her face. When the phone rang, she handed me the knife and pointed to the cucumber, and answered the phone in the living room. I always hated cucumber, so I put most of it back in the fridge, listening to Lil. I could tell by her voice that it was Grandmother Duncan on the other end, and by the way she said little more than "yes" and "no" and "everything's fine now."

"Grandmother Duncan wonders if you can go over sometime during the holidays and help her rebuild Buckingham Palace."

"You didn't tell her it was me?"

"I didn't have to. She guessed as soon as she saw it all. I know what you think of Grandmother Duncan"—and here I saw the first real smile on Lil's face for days, it seemed like—"but you have to realize there's a sharp brain inside that talking head."

She divided the lamb chops and mashed potatoes between two plates and carried them to the table in the living room. I followed with the salad. My face felt hot.

We ate for a while in silence. ST dragged herself out of her basket and tottered over to the table, nose twitching at the smell of the chops.

"Will she tell the cops?"

"Of course not. Look, Ian, the best way for you to deal with this particular problem is to go over there as soon as possible and apologize. Can't you see they're making a kind gesture—trying to be understanding?"

"More likely she doesn't want her friends knowing

there's yet another criminal in the family." They were going to find out anyway, I realized.

Lil sighed. "That sounded like a Gideon comment."

"It wasn't," I snapped. I wondered whether from now on, every time I said something Lil didn't like, she'd dig at me about Gideon.

"Okay. I'm sorry."

I knew it was going to be really hard to face the Duncans.

Lil was continuing. "She also asked about the cut on your forehead, and said I should complain to the gym." She smiled. "I didn't tell her that you'd been nowhere near the gym that night, but it got me thinking. Tell me again. It happened when you fell off the bus after the holdup, right?"

"Yes."

"And it must have been bleeding still quite a lot when you got back here. I saw your pillowcase. So if you'd gone on after the bus holdup to the car burning scene, you'd have had an obvious new cut on your face."

"So the guy whose car was burned must have noticed it. Did he say that in his description?"

"I don't know."

"If he didn't, it'll prove I wasn't there!"

"Don't get your hopes up, Ian. It might just prove it was too dark to see properly."

"If it was that dark, how could he describe me at all? Let's ask those detectives!"

"You want me to phone them now?"

"Don't phone. They're outside in a car watching the house."

"Really?" Lil went over and twitched the blind aside. "So they are. You wait here." She turned on the outside light and went.

I waited impatiently. I needed proof that I wasn't at

the car burning. I thought it through all over again. The gunman who had taken my gym bag knew what I looked like. He had to be connected with the car burning in some way if my gym bag turned up there. But it was the owner of the car who had given my description, not one of the burners. He had to be lying. Otherwise I couldn't make sense of it.

Then I heard loud voices from outside. In a second, Lil was inside, slamming the front door, leaning against it, breathing heavily. Her cheeks were bright red and her eyes angry and tearful. She leaned forward, clutching her middle.

"Lil—what's the matter? You want me to call a doctor?"

She shook her head, and then took two long quivering breaths. "It's just . . . I am so angry, for a moment I couldn't breathe."

She went into the living room and sat by the phone. I looked out the front. "Ian, you stay away from those windows!" She was angry, all right. But I'd seen enough to know that the plainclothes car had gone.

She was talking on the phone. "Get me Detective Inspector Tring. Oh. Well, get me that shaved one, what's his name, Detective Samuels." She tapped her nails on the sideboard as she waited. Her face was still flaming. "Oh, Detective Samuels. It's Lilian Ganty here." I could see her struggle to regain her calm. "There's a man watching my house and he's making threats against me and my grandson. . . . What does it matter what kind of threats? All you need to know is that he's frightening us and I want him arrested! . . . I know you detectives think it's far more interesting to go around trying to pin crimes on children, but it seems if you're faced with real grown-up crime . . ."

She stopped. She had lost the battle to stay calm. "No,"

she was shouting, "I don't know what make of car it was! It's pitch black outside!"

"Lil," I said, shaking her arm. I pointed at my scar. "Descriptions—remember?"

She glared at me for a couple of seconds, and then, quite suddenly, seemed to collect herself. "Ian . . . um . . . Ian has thought of some things which might help about the . . . the inquiries you're making. And we'd like to see the descriptions of him, please." She was quiet for a moment, listening, saying "mm" occasionally. Then, "Thank you." She hung up the receiver gently, and leaned back in her chair with her hands on her face.

"Lil . . . what's the matter? You went berserk back there!"

"It's Friday, isn't it? I want a . . . no, maybe not. I'll have a triple coffee instead."

"Lil! What's going on?"

"The detectives are coming back in the morning. They're bringing some photos to see if you recognize the bus holdup guy. And they're bringing the descriptions of you."

"Good. That's great. But that's not what I meant. What about the guy outside?"

"Oh, Ian, don't remind me." She groaned and covered her face again. "Why did I have to tell the cops about him? I just got so furious I lost it. Screeched like a ten-year-old."

"Hey. Don't insult ten-year-olds." I thought a feeble joke might help.

She didn't even hear. "How *dare* he? Coming here and threatening, making demands—" She was getting angry again.

"Who?" I shouted.

"Ian," she said, "it's Dan Kinnard. Pat's father. He's out of jail and he's tracked me down."

Photos

It was Saturday morning, and the police were back.

"He's on parole, Ms. Ganty. He's free to go anywhere, almost, as long as he reports regularly. We knew he was in town, of course. We just didn't know of his connection, er, with you."

Both detectives were looking at me as if this was a really illuminating aspect to my criminal behavior. I could see why Lil was angry with herself for bringing Dan Kinnard to their attention.

"We picked him up last night," Detective Inspector Tring was continuing, "and gave him a gentle warning. I don't think he'll bother you anymore."

"How did he threaten you exactly, Ms. Ganty?" asked Detective Samuels.

It took Lil a while to answer. At last she said, "You just have to look at his previous record. His very existence is a threat."

This conversation was going on while I was supposed to

be concentrating on a big plastic folder filled with photos of surly faces. After two pages they all started to look the same. The conversation was more interesting. And anyway, how could I say what the gunman looked like? He'd been almost totally covered up.

The detectives had noticed I'd given up turning over the pages of mug shots. "I didn't see him properly," I said. "I only saw his eyes. They were black and glittery. Anyone's eyes look black and glittery in a mask."

Samuels took some photos out of his briefcase. There were six. He spread them across the table. The faces had ski masks like the gunman's. "Can't you see how different they look, even with most of their faces hidden?" he said.

They did look different. I closed my eyes, recalling those moments in the bus, trying to picture the gunman. The picture in my head was dominated by the barrel of the gun pointing at me.

"This is our problem, Ian," said Tring. "You were seen at the bus holdup, and you were seen at the car burning. But your accomplice at the car burning isn't the gunman from the holdup. He's described quite differently. So, did you meet up with some other criminal pal and go on to Mile End to do the car burning?"

"If Ian's such an accomplished criminal," Lil drawled, "how come he's so stupid as to leave a library book and his gym bag behind?"

"Exactly, Ms. Ganty," Tring drawled back. "Inexperience, do you think?"

I interrupted. "You've only got the car owner's word for who was at the burning. How do you know he was telling the truth?"

Tring and Samuels exchanged a glance in the way I was starting to recognize. I detected a glimmer of hope. "You're supposed to be looking at those photos," said Samuels.

I went back to concentrating on the picture inside my

closed eyes. I opened them slightly and looked at the blurred images on the table. "That's him," I said. And I was sure.

Samuels put the other five photos back in his briefcase.

"Do you know who he is?" I asked.

"We do," said Tring. "And that's the identikit photo from the bus driver's description. So you and the driver agree."

"What about the descriptions of me? You were supposed to bring the photos of me!"

"Is he always this keen on seeing pictures of himself?" Samuels said to Lil in a jovial tone. She narrowed her eyes at him.

He handed over a photo. It was me, there was no doubt, even though I looked so stupid. My eyes were wide and idiotic. "Here's another one." This one was maybe me. I liked it. My hair looked quite good. Neither of them showed the cut on my face.

"So where did . . . Who . . . ?" I couldn't work out my question.

Samuels told me that the first one came from the bus driver's description. The second came from the car burning victim.

I rushed around the table and hugged Lil. "You see? You see? I wasn't there!"

Lil hugged me back. "It's proof," she said over my head to the detectives, "that Ian wasn't at the car burning. He got that cut on his face right after the bus incident. And believe me, there was plenty of blood. It must have been very obvious. You couldn't not notice it."

"It's not really proof, is it?" Samuels said. "After all, you've only got his word for it that he got the cut when he said he did. He didn't go to a doctor, did he? Like he didn't go to the police after the bus holdup."

Lil closed her eyes and sighed.

"And, Ms. Ganty, how did you know there was plenty of blood? What time did you see him that night?"

"Pillowcase," Lil said faintly. I was starting to feel alarmed.

"We're interested in those threats you mentioned. Are you sure you don't want to tell us about them?"

"No," said Lil in the same faint voice.

"We had quite a long talk with Mr. Kinnard. He'd been watching your house for several days. Ever since he arrived in Adelaide. Since Monday afternoon. I'm not surprised you were concerned."

"Look," I shouted. "If you're trying to hint around the fact that I was here on my own while Lil was away, well, it's not her fault. I was supposed to stay with our cousins. I just didn't so it's my fault. Not Lil's. She looks after me really well and I'm not going to be taken away to any other grandparents, so stop trying to set her up!"

I realized with horror that I was almost in tears but I forced my voice to keep going. "And I didn't have anything to do with that car burning. The car owner's lying!"

"Actually, we agree with you," Tring said. I couldn't believe his words at first, but his face was serious. He wasn't joking. "We suspected he might have been lying all along. The man's got a record of insurance fraud. But you and your gym bag kept popping up all over the place, complicating things."

"Then," Samuels took over, "we got our big break-through. It was our talk with Mr. Kinnard last night. He saw you arrive home on Tuesday night before eight, your face streaming with blood, he said." Samuels's voice changed slightly, as if he were mimicking. "A boy coming home all bloodied up to an empty house, he said. He waited for two hours, wondering whether to go in and make sure you were all right."

"Stop it!" Lil was on her feet. "Stop copying that

phony Irish accent and making the boy believe that his grandfather cares the slightest bit about him!"

"His grandfather?" echoed Samuels. "Really? He didn't tell us that. He just said he was a boyfriend of yours."

I hated them. They were playing with Lil. "Stop it!" I shouted in my turn.

Tring saw the look on my face. "We're sorry," he said. "Ms. Ganty, whether you like it or not, Mr. Kinnard—without having any idea of the cases we were working on—provided an alibi for your grandson and cleared him of the accusation of being involved in this car torching business."

Lil was sitting down again, her face hard.

Tring continued. "It was unfortunate Ian was caught up in the bus holdup. The driver agrees matters might have been as Ian describes them. The driver had just picked up a big win at the racetrack that afternoon. Obviously that was what the holdup was about."

"So what happened then?" I asked.

"Our gunman had another job to do that night. It seems he met the car owner and they torched the car. He left your gym bag at the scene and described you, so all the car owner had to do was report this whole made-up story to the police. He described you, Ian, and someone else out of his imagination—someone who looked very different from his real accomplice. And he claimed there were thousands of dollars' worth of property in the car lost in the fire."

"He burned his own car and blamed *me*?"

"Such outraged innocence," said Samuels, looking at the ceiling. "There still remains the matter of the stolen car and the joyride."

"Maybe you're mistaken there as well," said Lil.

"Well, Ian, did you hop in that car with your dog and drive off?"

Three pairs of eyes were watching me. I could deny it. I could say that ST jumped into the car—she was notorious for doing that—and if my fingerprints were there, well, I had to grab the steering wheel when I leaned in to get her, didn't I? Someone else came along later and took the car. After all, its keys were in the ignition, the door wide open.

Then they'd go on trying to prove it was me. I'd have to be fingerprinted. The questions and lying wouldn't end.

Gideon would have denied the whole thing. In fact, I could almost see his disbelieving face as I slowly nodded. "It was really stupid," I said. Lil reached over and squeezed my hand.

They spent some time telling me just how stupid it was. By the time they were finished, I was thinking I'd been lucky to drive half a block without smashing myself and six other people to pieces. Then Lil said, "So what happens now?"

Tring said that they had a new system to deal with cases like this. "Basically, the victim of the crime confronts the criminal."

"Confronts?" said Lil. "What do you mean?"

"Confronts . . . well, the idea is they talk together. The criminal's supposed to get some idea of the victim's point of view. They work out together a reasonable repayment for the crime."

"So," said Detective Inspector Tring, "you probably won't have to see us again. A social worker will arrive this afternoon at three o'clock to set up the meeting with the victim." He held out the two identikit photos of me. "Do you want these for your album?"

Repayment

I **was apprehensive** about this meeting with the social worker. So was Lil. I could tell by the way she was ironing the dish towels over and over, and by the way she kept on reassuring me.

"They'll probably just want you to pay for his body shop costs. Maybe make up in some way for the inconvenience of being without his car. Don't be nervous, Ian."

"I'm not."

"Anyway, the social worker's only coming here to set up a meeting."

"How much does body repair cost?"

"Heaps. You'll have to figure out some way to earn money. Maybe over the summer break."

I felt gloomy. What job could I possibly get? This repayment could be hanging around for years.

The time was creeping along. "Why don't you fill in the next hour or so by going to see the Grandparents Duncan? Get it over with," Lil suggested.

"It's too hard, right now," I said. I had plenty of straightforward, rational reasons for disliking the Duncans. For instance, they'd never wanted me to be alive anyway, they made Pat and Elaine go to America, and Grandfather Duncan had pretended to like Pat and then called him a feckless bugger. These were all things I should have been able to say to them. But smashing Buckingham Palace and scrawling red words on their garage doors—well, it was so humiliating. That was what I resented about Gideon. Everything he'd made me do was stupid. Nothing better than I could have thought up for myself.

"I'll go and see the Duncans after the social worker has gone," I said, but Lil wasn't listening. She collected the piles of ironing and headed for her room. I turned on the TV, flicked through the channels, watched a local news-flash to make sure I hadn't done anything else I didn't remember. And then looked at Lil, who'd returned to the living room. She'd changed her clothes.

Her jeans were ironed and she had on a cream silk shirt with big sleeves. A long scarf was flung around her neck. At first I thought it was new, but then I realized I must have seen it before. Dark purple with jet beads embroidered into its fringe.

I took a deep breath. "You look terrific."

"I thought I'd better look respectable for the social worker," she said. She fiddled with her scarf ends and I remembered Gideon's curses when their jet beads blinded him.

The door knocker sounded and ST tumbled out of her basket, barking. Lil stood, then sat down again. "Surely it's too early for the social worker. Can you get the door, Ian?"

She was right. It wasn't the social worker. It took me a second to realize that the man standing outside the door was Pat's father, Dan Kinnard. He was smiling widely at me, a medium-sized, middle-aged man with a balding head and glasses and a long neck. A little like Pat but not really. He had Pat's smile.

"Hello, Ian," he said. "I'm Danny."

"You!" It was an explosion from Lil behind me.

"Come on now, Lil. You have to invite me in. Even your little dog likes me."

"ST likes everyone," Lil said sourly. "The police said you wouldn't be bothering us again."

"I'm here with the blessing of the police," Dan Kinnard said. "I'm here to chat to the lad who borrowed my car."

I was astounded, couldn't speak, and nor could Lil for a moment or two, but after that there wasn't much she could do but grudgingly let him come in.

He said that he'd known the name of the street we lived on, but not the house number. "I was in the phone booth less than a minute looking in the book, and zoom! Off went my car."

"You wouldn't have found us in the book," Lil said. "We're unlisted."

"So I had to borrow a car for a couple of days while the police went over mine with magnifying glasses or whatever they do. In the end I told them not to bother. The lad had the car with my permission. He's welcome to it anytime." He was looking at me as he spoke.

"Don't you dare try to bribe him!" shouted Lil. "He's too young to get a license anyway."

He turned to her. "Would you offer me a cup of tea?"

"No. So how did you track me down?"

"It wasn't like that, Lil. I came to visit you and Ian. You see, Pat invited me."

I heard Lil gasp. "Pat," she whispered. "How . . . How . . ."

I felt cold and there were goose bumps on my arms.

"Pat wrote to me. A couple of years ago. He and his wife were filling in time, waiting at Sydney airport for their connection to Hawaii." He shook his head. "It was amazing. Suddenly I find I have a son and a daughter-in-law, and not only that, a grandson. It made a huge, huge difference to my life."

Lil was recovering from her shock. "I suppose you're going to try and tell me you're a changed man," she said.

"You might not be ready to believe it till your dying day, Lilian Ganty, but everyone else believes it. Do you think I'd be walking around a free man if they didn't believe it? Do you think those detectives would have sent me here this afternoon if they didn't believe it? I've got a job to start next week. I've got most of a university degree finished."

"A degree?" Lil laughed. "With a major in pyramid selling, no doubt."

I found my voice. "What did Pat say in the letter?"

"He told me all about you, boyo," Dan Kinnard said. "He said the trip to the States was a real new start for him and Elaine, a last chance to make the marriage a good one. But he said the only black spot on the rose was leaving their darling boy at home." He glanced at Lil. "It was like only the day after I got this letter I read in the paper about the air accident. I had a son for a day. But I still had a grandson. So I got busy."

The room seemed full of the presence of Pat. I could picture him at the airport, writing his letter, not knowing that this warm gesture to his unknown father would bring Dan Kinnard here, now, this week, this most dangerous week of my life. Because that's how I was feeling, then; rescued just in time. He'd appeared when I needed help to deal with the consequences of Gideon, that overwhelming specter of my imagination.

Lil's ice rarely melted during the hours Dan Kinnard

stayed talking to us, through several cups of tea, and later, dinner; even when he flirted with her it was as if his words skated over her head. She was polite to him, and that was as far as she'd go. Only when she spoke about Pat did she drop her coldness.

I told him about the Grandparents Duncan. "They're very . . . respectable people," I said.

"Not the sort to enjoy graffiti all over their house, I can see that."

"Not *all* over. Just the garage doors." I felt uncomfortable with this memory, and also because I knew I still had to face them. I noticed this was one of the times that Dan Kinnard glanced at Lil, as if inviting her to collude with him in teasing me; but once again, it was as if she didn't notice.

"But why 'body snatcher'?"

I shrugged. I hardly knew the real version of the story myself and had no idea what train of reasoning had led me-as-Gideon to scrawl those words. Here Lil came to my rescue. "It's an old story," she said, "and one that Pat found irresistibly funny." Lil couldn't stop herself from laughing. "He wouldn't leave it alone, no matter how upset Elaine got about his jokes. It was just a terrible mix-up at the Duncans' funeral business. A casket turned up at a funeral service without the body inside. The relatives discovered this by pure accident. The body was still back in the fridge at the funeral parlor. Then everybody who'd had a Duncan funeral started to worry. Was there really a body inside that casket that the reverend had been blessing before it went into the oven? Or was Auntie Nelly still in the back of some freezer? Or worse, sold off to a hospital for body parts? The stories went on and on. People got hysterical."

"That's crazy. Surely people know who they're burying."

"Well, that's just it. Often they don't. Lots of people

don't see the body ever again from the time the doctor pronounces death and the funeral directors take the dead person away. It's the modern way. People like death to be hidden."

This was the longest conversation Lil and Dan Kinnard had together. After that, Lil sort of closed down again. Dan said to me he would come with me to see the Grandparents Duncan. We'd face them together. "We'll go over to their place on Monday," he said, "right after lunchtime. Monday's a good and sensible working day. Just made for sorting out problems."

It was getting late. Dan Kinnard left. I noticed Lil only touched his fingers when he offered a handshake as he went. "I really like him," I said to her.

"That's up to you. You're old enough to make your own mind up about that. Just leave me out of it."

"You must have liked him once."

"It was always a mistake. Don't think it was some romantic teenage love affair between Dan Kinnard and me that brought Pat into the world. It was not. Far from it." The way she said it stopped me asking more about that.

"You don't mind if he comes with me on Monday?"

"As I said, it's up to you."

Rebuilding

It wasn't up to me. Dan, it seemed, was destined to be part of our lives only at crucial times. The phone rang that Monday morning; it was Dan, calling from Alice Springs. He was on the way to find out about another job. He wished me the very best of luck and said he looked forward to seeing me "next time."

"Surprise, surprise," said Lil when I told her I'd be going to the Duncans' without Dan Kinnard. But that was all she said. She didn't say "told you so" or anything like that.

So I had to face the Grandparents Duncan on my own. I did feel very alone, walking up to their front door—no Gideon, and even Jacqueline seemed to belong to another story.

Grandmother Duncan answered the door. "Ian," she said, neither pleased nor unpleased. No "darling," though. Was this a good sign or not? When I thought about it later, I decided it was a good thing. It meant she saw me as a real person, and, in fact, she's hardly ever called me darling again.

But back to that hard first visit. She led me to the dining room. On this bright spring morning, the house was full of sunshine. The coins were in an orange plastic bucket beside the tray holding the crumbled remains of Buckingham Palace. I looked away from them immediately, feeling awkward. "Here's the plan for you to follow," said Grandmother Duncan. The plan was as much use to me as a knitting pattern. It was on the puzzle page of an old English newspaper and looked like a nightmare of tiny circles. Still, there was a drawing of the finished construction, and I thought that might be of some help. "I'll bring you a coffee in a little while. Turn on the radio or the TV, if you like." Then she left the room. At least she wasn't going to stand around waiting for me to beg her for forgiveness or something.

I worked impatiently at first, hating the way the coins slithered and teetered. I learned it was better to build up the piles of coins evenly around the whole building. The complicated plans started to make some sense. I could work out which parts of the base needed double or even triple walls of coins to strengthen the construction. After an hour, I was getting a glimmer of how some people might even enjoy this sort of activity. After two hours, I would have strangled anyone who messed up my beautiful building.

It was Grandfather Duncan who brought me the coffee. It was on a tray covered by a white cloth still showing crisp ironed folds. There was a small jug of milk and a bowl with sugar in it, and a plate holding a soft, spongy little cake crusted with pale icing. "She's sure all boys like cakes," he said. He put the tray on the coffee table and then sat on one of the dining room chairs. "A remarkable woman, I've always thought. Knows what's what about everything."

I added milk to the coffee, and sugar, and stirred it for a while. I saw the small fork beside the cake and the embroidered napkin.

"Usually she does, anyway. Your recent exploits shook her up a bit."

Here it comes, I thought. I glanced at his face, then looked back. He didn't seem angry. "I'm really sorry, Grandfather," I started to say.

He went right on as if he hadn't heard. "I said to her, she shouldn't expect people always to be how she decides they are. I mean, she should remember how Elaine suddenly stopped being a buttoned-up student teacher and fell for your dad. Insisted on sticking by him." He shook his head. "I didn't say that to her. About Elaine, I mean. She still grieves too much for Elaine. We both do." He looked at me. "You too, I know."

"Yes. But that's not why . . ." I had to start again. "I don't know why all those things happened. I just . . ."

"Nobody knows. I remember being fourteen and fifteen, and they were the worst years of my life. You'll survive." He stood up. "Don't let your coffee get cold," he said, and then he was gone.

The cake was delicious. I worked away at the palace until the sun had left the room and Grandmother Duncan was there, asking if I wanted lunch. My fingers were black from the coins.

"I'll come back tomorrow," I said. "I'll probably get it finished."

"See you in the morning, then, Ian," she said, and I pecked her cheek swiftly and left.

• • •

"She made this fantastic little cake for me," I told Lil. "I ate it all."

"Ask her for the recipe," said Lil. "Cook one for me."

• • •

I still didn't know how to put things right with Jaz. I missed her very much, but I realized it would take lots of time before she'd forgive me and let me tell her about Gideon. It was this need to explain to Jaz that led me to nudge the corpse of Gideon to see what would happen.

I found I could breathe life into him as I needed, enough to write his story over again. This time, he stayed on the page. I've been able to control him.